GHOST AUDIT

JULIE PARKER

This is a work of fiction. Names, characters, places, and incidents are products of the author's imagination or are used fictitiously and are not to be construed as real. Any resemblance to actual events, locations, organizations, or persons, living or dead, is entirely coincidental.

World Castle Publishing, LLC
Pensacola, Florida
Copyright © 2023 Julie Parker
Paperback ISBN: 9798891260641
eBook ISBN: 9798891260658
First Edition World Castle Publishing, LLC, October 16, 2023
http://www.worldcastlepublishing.com

Licensing Notes

Cover: Karen Fuller
Editor: Karen Fuller

For Brad & Cam, my boys

CHAPTER 1

This had to be the worst day of my life. Or, at least, right up there with one of the worst.

The man seated behind the desk before me scrutinized my file, and every few minutes, he would look up and give me a little smirk. Being audited was bad enough, but this was downright insulting.

"So, you make your living as a ghostbuster?"

At least he managed to say it with a straight face.

"Paranormal Investigator. Mr. Tarland, do I really need to be here for this? I only came by to drop this stuff off to you. I never expected to come in for a sit down."

"Miss Marshall, I would think being here would be in your best interest. I have a lot of questions regarding the deductions you've calculated."

"What kind of questions? I run a business. I have a home office." I waved my hand, indicating my files. "These are everyday normal expenses one can expect."

"Normal expenses for an abnormal line of work."

"Granted, this is an unusual kind of business, but I do offer a legitimate service."

"Busting ghosts?"

"Bringing peace to the dead and closure to the living."

"Most businesses have revenue."

"There is modest income. I've only been up and running for about eighteen months. My website had some problems, and I had to bring in someone to redo it. That costs money. Not to mention the expense of the start-up equipment I needed."

"Yes, I can see that." He lifted a

document and perused the contents. "Infrared camera, motion detectors, video cameras, back-up battery packs, tape recorder. What's EVP?"

"Electronic voice phenomenon."

"For eavesdropping on ghostly conversations?"

I didn't care for the way he wiggled his fingers about when he said that. "I'm not the only person in this line of work."

"I know. Hamilton is full of charlatans telling fortunes and pagan shops selling good luck charms, magic potions, and hex bags."

"Not everyone dealing with the paranormal is a fraud. I have a long list of satisfied customers. I'd be more than happy to get signed statements for you."

"No need to get upset, Miss Marshall."

What a haughty ass he was, sitting there all big, handsome, and pompous behind his desk. I bet he expected me to swoon all over him. Just because he worked for the government, he thought he could get away with his condescending attitude. If he thought he was intimidating me, he was mistaken. Just two nights ago, I'd faced down what felt like the devil himself in a cemetery full of witnesses out on a ghost walk. Gained quite a few customers in the process.

"Once word gets out, I'm sure business will pick up, and by next year you'll be more than happy to take half of everything I make."

That wiped the smug smile off his face.

"The government isn't out to get you, contrary to popular belief."

"Now, who's guilty of peddling bull?"

He leaned forward suddenly, giving me a deadly glare. With his obvious monstrous height and bulging muscles, I admit, for half a second, I almost felt intimidated.

Almost.

I faced him down. "Are we finished here?"

Engaged in a stare-off, he finally broke the spell and looked up over my head toward his closed office door. I couldn't help but wonder if he wanted to pull out the thumbscrews but was afraid the room wasn't soundproof.

"No, not yet," he said.

"I don't know what else you want from me. I could have just mailed this stuff to you, but I went out of my way to drive downtown to drop it off in person. My parking meter is probably expired, and all I have to show for my diligence is insults and probably a parking ticket."

"If you feel insulted, that wasn't my intention."

Was that contrition I heard in his voice?

"And if you have a parking ticket, bring it to me, and I'll take care of it for you."

"Now, isn't that nice?" I fairly oozed

sarcasm.

"Like I said, I'm not out to get you. I have a job to do. One that's not nearly as exciting as yours, I'm sure."

"Is that a wisecrack?"

"No. Why are you so defensive?"

I let out a big sigh and leaned back in my chair. He was right, I was being defensive, but he *had* been an ass. "Mr. Tarland…."

"Call me Pete."

Oh, so we're on a first name basis now, are we? "Ok, Pete, then. If you find me defensive, then you and your ghost-busting jokes are the reason why. It's not just you. I get slack from a lot of people. Nonbelievers, I like to call them."

"You can't expect everyone to believe in ghosts."

"I don't. But can they be disproved?"

"In many cases, yes, they can. Noisy plumbing, settling houses, wild animals, combined with overactive imaginations, makes for many a ghostly tale."

"Sure, plenty of them can be debunked. But just as many of them can't."

"Tell me, Phoebe—may I call you Phoebe?"

I didn't like it, but I nodded my head anyway.

"Have you ever seen a ghost?" he asked. His shoulder-length brown hair brushed against the collar of his black suit jacket. The jacket itself seemed too tight to contain his arms. He steepled his hands beneath his chin while his dazzling blue eyes bore into me, creating an uncomfortable heat in my body.

"More than I can count."

"Really?"

He seemed genuinely interested, so I answered him. "Yes, I've seen ghosts ever since I was a little girl."

"Well, I have a proposition for you."

That definitely intrigued me. "A proposition?" Was he going to forgo the audit if I agreed to fool around with him in a spooky mansion? I'd have to give it great consideration before I accepted.

"I want to come along with you the next time you have a job. I want to see exactly what it is you do."

"From a strictly business point of view?" I was fishing, but I couldn't help it.

"Of course."

"Then you'll be satisfied? The government will allow my business expenses for being a paranormal investigator?"

"I can't make any guarantees, but it would help your case immensely."

I smiled and got to my feet. "Then I accept. The next big case I go on, you can tag along."

Pete stood up and reached out his hand for me to shake. His grip was firm, and it wasn't my imagination that he held me just a little longer than necessary. When he let go, he snapped up one of his business cards off his desk and passed it to me. He took a moment and wrote another number on the back of the card.

"That's my home number. If it's after hours, you can reach me there. Don't forget to call," he said as I walked out his office door.

How *ever* could I forget?

Chapter 2

Being after seven o'clock on a Friday night, I thought it safe to don my jammies and convalesce on the couch with a huge bowl of popcorn. It'd been the week from hell, and all I wanted was a quiet evening to myself.

Since my audit on Monday, the week had steadily declined. Tuesday, my car got a flat tire going out of town to look at a job—a big one—making me arrive almost an hour late and appearing completely unprofessional. Wednesday, I must have gotten twenty calls from the same creep, absolutely determined he had a naked ghost of Marilyn Monroe in his bedroom and that I needed to get her out quick before his mother got home. Thursday, I drove to the edge of town to investigate a dilapidated shed on the back forty of an old woman's property. It used to serve as her husband's hidey-hole, and she reported seeing strange lights and hearing country tunes coming from that location late in the evenings. The shed was so run-down I had to measure every step I took to prevent breaking through the rotted wooden floor. When I finally found the poor old ghost-man, I didn't know who was more shocked, him or me. An hour later, after promising to give messages to all his loved ones, he finally agreed to move on and rest in peace.

Which brought me to today. I'd been offered a job, which could be a good thing or a bad thing. The problem was that it was the big old house—the one I was late checking out on Tuesday. I got the call back in the morning. Janet, the woman who owned the house, apparently sold it to some hotshot developer, and when he heard the rumors about it being haunted, he was far from daunted. He loved the idea of it. He was thinking of turning the place into a B&B—a *haunted* B&B. It was all the rage nowadays, apparently. Janet, who still occupied the property, found out about the man's intentions and was freaking out. She's the one who called and hired me. It being near the end of October, Janet must vacate the premises by the end of the month. Until then, I had to get rid of the ghost, or should I say ghosts? Three of them, it seemed. Lovers who died tragically a hundred years ago. It was an unsolved mystery of what had transpired. Possibly, the pair had been murdered by a third party—that being the other ghost on the property. Janet had told me all about the ghosts and the house while she gave me the grand tour on Tuesday. She failed to inform me about the new owner and his plans until this morning after I accepted the job.

That put me in a pickle.

The haunted B&B — which the old house is being turned into — would generate business if there were ghosts. Since the place was being touted as such, the developer would be mighty annoyed if he realized he was suddenly minus a few spooks. I dearly wanted to cross the ghosts over, but if the new owner discovered what I was about, it could be very bad for business. What if he threatened to sue for the loss of ghosts?

I leaned back into the soft cushions of the couch and pulled my blanket up around me. On the TV was a murder mystery movie, and when it flashed to a scene of a big fellow sitting smugly behind a desk, it reminded me of Pete Tarland. Technically, I should have called him when I went out on my next job, which was the one with the old man in the back forty. I'd not been in the mood for company, though, and I'd also been in a bit of a hurry, so the thought hadn't crossed my mind until I was driving home again. Even if I had invited him along on that job, it wouldn't have gone a long way in convincing him I was legit. Pete wouldn't have been able to see the ghost—most people can't—especially with him being a nonbeliever, so it would have just been him sitting around watching me talk to air. How exciting.

But perhaps he'd be interested in the haunted B&B job?

Janet said there was a lot of goings-on in the house, so if Pete saw some stuff he genuinely couldn't explain, maybe he'd consider the possibility of ghosts?

Yes, I'd take him with me, as long as he was willing to start Monday. It was a big house and could be a big job. I would probably need at least a night or two. Most of my tracking was done between the hours of midnight and three AM. We could sleep in the daytime. Janet had offered to give me a bedroom or two to use as I needed. Just so long as I had things wrapped up by the end of the month.

Having made my mind up, I climbed off the couch and went to retrieve Pete's business card. I took it off my fridge, where I'd pinned it with a magnet shaped like a ghost. Grabbing the phone, I sat down at my two-seater kitchen table, not wanting to be curled up on the couch while I talked to Mr. Muscles.

After I dialed the number on the back of the card, I waited. Three rings, four, five.... *When would the darn voicemail pick up?* I'd kind of expected him to be home on a Friday night. He didn't seem the type to loosen up even a little. After seven rings, I was about to give up, irritated that he probably was too cheap to invest in a digital mailbox. Then he surprised me by snapping up the phone and hollering, "What?"

The phone had been away from my ear, and I had almost hung up, but he'd spoken so loudly that I'd heard him. Now, I listened but didn't say anything. Perhaps I should just hang up, considering how annoyed he sounded? With my luck, he had a call display, and he'd call back. I did have voicemail on my phone, and I didn't know how to deactivate it, so even if I didn't pick up, he'd still know I'd called.

Then he'd really be mad.

"Um, hi, Pete?"

"Yeah?" Still angry.

"It's me, Phoebe. Remember from Monday?"

He paused for a moment, then, "Oh, yeah, I remember. Ghost girl."

Still the same ass. "That's me. Ah, you wanted to go along with me on a job, remember?"

"You got one?"

The surprise in his voice irritated me. "Yeah, a big one, in fact. Huge old house outside of town. I'm gonna leave Monday, around ten. Do you want to go?"

"Ten in the morning?"

"Yep. And it's probably gonna be an overnighter or possibly a couple of days."

Another pause. I could hear some papers rustling. "Ah, okay. I'll have to switch a few things around and maybe bring my laptop to work remotely. Can you pick me up?"

So, no voicemail and no car. No wonder he was after my money. "I guess. Just give me directions."

"Can you pick me up at Leon's Book and Coffee shop on...."

"I know where it is."

"Great, I'll see you Monday then, at ten."

"Yeah, okay. Make sure you pack for a couple of nights' stay, just in case." I hung up the phone thinking it was going to be anything but great to spend days out of town in a big old, haunted house with a government auditor. This job had the potential to make or break me. I really needed those business expense write-offs.

When I climbed into bed around nine, I was still thinking about Pete. He was big and handsome but such a jerk. He'd probably spend the entire time smirking about the whole ghost thing. I crossed my fingers and made a wish that something big would happen next week. Something that would scare the crap out of Mr. Smartypants.

Chapter 3

Pete was checking out the bookshelves when I arrived to pick him up. He noticed me standing in line waiting for coffee and saddled over. "Want coffee?" I asked him.

"Sure, but I'll get it. Least I can do considering you're driving."

"No sense taking two vehicles." I shrugged. "Mine's got all the equipment in it."

"Gonna put all those write-offs to use, are you?"

He sounded sarcastic, so I ignored him. We got our coffees and walked out to my car. He tossed his duffle bag into the back seat and then folded himself into the front seat of my jeep, sliding it back as far as it would go.

"Comfy?" My turn to be sarcastic, his turn to ignore me.

The drive took over an hour. The first fifteen minutes were filled with stilted conversation. The rest consisted of uncomfortable silence except for the sounds of the radio. Finally, when I'd turned off the two-lane highway onto a gravel road, and we were about five minutes away, I began to fill him in on the job.

"The house we're going to was sold to a developer who's hoping to turn it into a Bed and Breakfast."

"Does he know it's supposedly haunted?"

"He does. That's the allure. He wants to open a haunted B&B." I figured I might as well tell Pete everything. If there was some sort of conflict of interest, he might know what to do about it.

"What's the problem, then? Why call

in a ghost buster if he likes it the way it is?"

"The current owner, Janet, has possession of the house until the end of the month. She didn't know about the man's intentions to turn the house into a haunted B&B until recently after she had sold it."

"There's no law against it."

"No. But she feels betrayed anyway. She told him about the ghosts, and now she's upset he's going to exploit them."

"Exploit the ghosts?"

Why did he have to be such a jerk? Ghosts had feelings too. "Yes, that's why she hired me to move them along."

"Cross them over?" When I raised an eyebrow at him, he explained. "I've seen Ghost Whisperer a couple of times."

"Good show. And yes, I plan on crossing them over."

"We're not all going to cry at the end, are we?"

Prick.

Soon I was turning onto the long

straight driveway, which had huge old beautiful oaks in a line down either side of it. The lengthy, bowed branches formed a canopy over the dirt road, practically blocking out the sun and making it look like we'd entered a tunnel. The first time I'd driven down here, I'd wondered if when I got to the end, I'd be transported back in time. I could almost hear the sounds of carriages pulled by horses trouncing down the same laneway.

I pulled up before the house and climbed out of the jeep. Pete got out and stretched his legs. The amazed expression on his face made me smile.

"They sure don't make 'em like this anymore," he said.

"Nope."

He noticed me opening the back door of the jeep and hauling out some of my equipment. Without asking, he opened the other side and began to help. He put a bag and tripod onto the ground at his feet and stared up at the enormous dwelling. There were three floors, the third being an attic.

"Would you call this gothic style?" He slung a bag over each broad shoulder and reached back into the jeep for more.

"I thought that too, at first. Janet said it's actually called Second Empire, popular back in the Victorian Age. This house was built in 1890. That's called a mansard roof." I pointed up to the attic.

"And that's a tower." He pointed to our left, where there was, in fact, a tower arched over the wide stairway.

"It looks cool from the inside. In the attic, there's a two-step staircase with a little handrail. You can climb up to the top of the tower to look out those big windows."

"That is cool."

"The house is also very secluded. It sits on a lot of land. The nearest neighbor is several acres away."

"Good, so there'll be no one to hear me scream," he said.

I drilled him with a warning look. "Very funny. If you do feel the need to run off in terror, then head down the driveway, not to the back of the house, 'cause there's a long narrow creek that travels right across the lawn. I wouldn't want you to fall in."

He gave me a goofy smile as though saying *Yeah, like that's gonna happen*.

We walked down the pathway and up the wide staircase to the double front doors. Shuffling around the bags I held in my hands, I rapped the old brass knocker a couple of times. A few moments later, I could hear some rustling inside.

"She's expecting us, right?"

Was that a worried frown marring the smooth perfect brow of my hunky companion?

"Yes," I assured him.

"What would you call this color?" He nodded his head in the direction of the painted wood siding of the house.

"I dunno. Green, I guess."

"That's what I thought. If you were to tell someone you spent the night in a green house, the first thing that'd pop into your mind would be 'tacky'. But this light green, with the darker green shutters and the burgundy trim, actually looks pretty good."

Agreeing with his assessment, I was about to say so when the door suddenly creaked open. Janet stood there, dressed in a faded yellow dress and white apron, her gray hair pulled back off her face.

"Phoebe, I'm so glad you could come out this week." She immediately turned her eyes on Pete. "And who is this? Your handsome fella come to keep you company?"

Pete cleared his throat and suddenly found the trim work on the porch fascinating.

"Ah, no. Janet, this is Pete. Pete, Janet." I introduced them. Pete turned his attention back to Janet and gave her a nod in greeting. "He's just helping me out."

"She needs someone to carry in all the heavy equipment," Pete supplied.

"Oh, how kind," Janet said, flashing a bright smile. She stepped back from the door and gestured us in. "Please, come in, come in. You can put all your bags into the front sitting room for now."

When we stepped inside, I noticed another set of bags sitting in the foyer. "Are you taking my advice, Janet, and staying at a friend's place for a while?" I hoped this was the case. It was much easier for me to do my job when I didn't have homeowners underfoot to worry about.

"Yes, dear. My good friend Lara is picking me up shortly. She lives just up the road a ways. I left her number on the kitchen table. You've toured the house, and you know all about Annie and John. You should do fine. I must say, though, I am so happy you'll have Pete here with you."

"Annie and John?" Pete asked.

"I'll explain later," I told him.

Honk, Honk!

"Oh, that'll be Lara." We looked

through the open door, and sure enough, an old Grand Marquis in mint condition was pulling up to park beside my jeep. "I've just baked a bunch of chocolate chip cookies — they're cooling on the stove. The fridge is packed full, so help yourselves. You have the number where I'll be, so I guess that's everything." She pulled a jacket from the hall closet and slipped into her shoes and headed for the door. When she turned back suddenly, remembering her bags, Pete had already put down my stuff and picked up hers. Janet eyed him with approval.

"What a fine gentleman you are." Pete blushed.

Soon, Janet's bags were stowed away in the trunk of the car, and Pete joined me on the porch to wave goodbye.

"Good luck!" Janet called out her open window as the car began to pull down the driveway.

Now the two of us were alone.

CHAPTER 4

It didn't take long for Annie and John to make their presence known. As soon as Pete and I stepped back through the double doors, both slammed shut behind us.

"Damn! That's some wind," Pete said.

"Yeah." He knew as well as I did that there was no wind. I picked my stuff up in the foyer and brought it into the sitting room where Janet had said to put it. It was a mid-size, comfortable room, sparsely furnished — as was the rest of the house, considering Janet's upcoming move — supplying ample room for us to spread out. Pete followed me in with the equipment.

"There's more in the jeep," he said,

putting down what he held. "Do you want me to bring it in now?"

Was it just me, or did it seem he was already antsy about being here?

"Sure, thanks."

It took him a while to come back in.

"There are seven bedrooms in this house, all of which are on the upper levels," I said as he put the rest of my gear down.

"Wow."

"Janet's been using an old sewing room on this floor as her bedroom for the past few years. The stairs became too much for her. You can have the first pick of which bedroom you'd like. I think only four of them have beds, though. The two bedrooms on the attic level are completely empty." *Not like he'd really choose to sleep in the attic.*

"The place seems deserted already. Your voice practically echoes."

"I know. Wait till you see the attic. Aside from the two bedrooms, the rest is just one giant room. Almost completely empty.

Janet said that's where a lot of the activity used to occur." I slung a camera bag over one shoulder and my overnight bag over the other. "Can you bring up the tripods? I want to set up two cameras in the attic."

"Sure." He picked up the two long bags holding the tripods but then stared at me intently. "Hey, if you can see ghosts, why do you need all this stuff?" The auditor in him suddenly reared its suspicious head. It'd only been a matter of time, I suppose.

"The equipment isn't for me. There're a lot of nonbelievers just like you out there, and they require proof. Even the ones who know without a doubt that something otherworldly is going on."

He shrugged. "People will always require proof of things they don't understand."

"That's why Big Foot, the Loch Ness Monster, and aliens are continually hunted."

"And ghosts."

"Yes, and ghosts. That's where I come

in."

"You and your write-offs."

Jerk.

We went up the stairs to the second floor and walked to the end of the hall to climb the staircase leading to the attic. Outside the last bedroom, I'd casually dropped my overnight bag. We'd passed several doors on the second floor, and while Pete set up the tripods, I wondered if he'd glimpsed any of the bedrooms. They were all a good size, each room being unique, offering a slightly different view of the grounds. I had a favorite already picked out from my last visit, closest to the attic staircase. I hoped Pete would choose something at the opposite end. The only full bathroom in the house was on the second floor and situated right in the middle of the hall, so we'd undoubtedly bump into each other sometime. There was a powder room on the main floor by the kitchen and another in the attic.

"I'm going to go to bed early tonight

and set my alarm for midnight. I suggest you do the same if you want to see anything."

"Ok, you're the expert. I've heard most hauntings occur during the wee hours of the morning."

"Yeah, between twelve and three, I've found." I fiddled with the cameras until they were set up the way I wanted, encompassing views of the room and set on motion detection. This would leave us free to explore other areas of the house. I had a handy-dandy handheld monitor that would light up if the motion detectors were triggered, alerting me to something going on. "This should do it for up here."

"Are you setting anything else up?" Pete asked.

"I only have these two cameras to set up stationery. If I could afford more, I'd set them up on each level of the house."

"Um, hum."

I knew he was thinking about my write-offs again. I could envision him with a notepad and pen jotting everything down. As I eyed him critically, I couldn't help but notice, to my annoyance, his good looks. Why he couldn't have just offered to make the entire audit go away by simply asking me out on a date was beyond me. I would've been up for it.

Perhaps he wasn't available? He didn't wear a ring, but lots of married guys didn't. Maybe there was a Mrs. Tarland? That would explain his obvious indifference to me. Although, I had to admit, if only to myself, I wasn't exactly emitting warm and fuzzy vibes toward him. His obnoxious demeanor made me bristly. Granted, he was here to do a job, and so was I. But if we put all that aside, I knew I would remain on high alert around him. My defensiveness stemmed from protecting myself from the disdain I ultimately experienced whenever dating. As soon as they got a glimpse into my paranormal world, they'd head for the hills. Some of them thought I was crazy. Others were afraid. Needless to say, romance had always been difficult for me.

I led the way downstairs and into the first bedroom—or the last, depending on how you looked at it. Using my foot, I'd slid my overnight bag the rest of the way through the door. "If you don't mind, I prefer this room. I'd like to be as close to the attic as possible."

Pete's eyes were on the queen-size bed sitting square in the middle of the floor. "Sure, no problem."

We left the room and strolled down the hall, checking out the other bedrooms along the way. When we reached the last bedroom, Pete stepped inside and went right over to the window, just as he'd done in each of the other rooms he'd considered—whether they'd had a bed in them or not. The large bay window looked out over the right side of the manor. Being a corner bedroom, as was the room I'd chosen, an identical window looked out over the front of the house, whereas mine looked over the left side and back of the house. I joined him at the window.

"Nice view," he said.

I nodded in agreement thinking this room probably had one of the nicest views.

"I think I'll take this one." He walked over to the double bed and sat down, giving a couple of bounces to check out the springs. The bed squeaked, but not too loudly. When he lay back, I turned my head away from him, hiding my suddenly flushed cheeks.

"Do you want something to eat?" I asked him.

"Sure. Why? You hungry?" Was that a suggestive tone in his voice, or was it just my imagination? When he got up off the bed and walked past me out the door, his face was neutral. I must have imagined it.

Chocolate chip cookies were on the stove, just as Janet had promised. They'd cooled down, but not enough that when I lifted one and broke it in half, the chips still oozed.

"Yum, my favorite," Pete said, already talking with his mouth full. I noticed he'd scooped three or four cookies into his hands.

"Mine too." I plucked a few more off the tray and set them down on the table. "Do you want milk?"

"Sure." He sat down while I rummaged through the cabinets, looking for cups. I poured us each a glass, then took the seat across from him. "We're breaking the rules, you know."

"Huh?"

"Eating dessert before lunch." He waved a cookie around while he spoke.

"Oh, yeah. Well, I'll make us some sandwiches if you like?"

"Ok, maybe just one, though, since you want to eat an early dinner. Hey, speaking of dinner…."

"Let me look." I got up and opened the fridge again. "There's a small, defrosted chicken, and we could have a salad with it." I wandered into the pantry. "Or there's potatoes and carrots in here."

"Sounds good. Can you cook, or do you want me to make it?"

"You cook?" This surprised me. Most of the guys I'd dated didn't even know what an oven looked like. Or else, they'd never stuck around long enough for me to find out.

"Sure. I'm a bachelor, so I've learned to fend for myself."

I went back to the table and sat down to finish my snack. *So, he was a bachelor, eh? Interesting.*

"What do you want to do this afternoon?" he asked.

"Oh, I'm sure we can think of something." I couldn't help but smile. The way he was licking the cookie crumbs off his fingers was having a devastating effect on me. Everything about this man—ass that he was—intrigued me. Once I could tear my eyes away from his mouth, I cleared my throat loudly.

"I guess I could show you around the rest of the house. We could walk the grounds too. Check out the creek I told you about."

"I don't want to bore you. I mean, if you've already seen it...."

I put up my hand to interrupt. "No. Janet only showed me around inside. I'd like to do some exploring."

"Okay, then."

Caught up in the excitement of exploration, we both forgot about having a sandwich. We strolled through the first floor while I gave Pete a run-down on the home's history, repeating what Janet had told me.

"So why does Janet believe ghosts live in her home?"

"Oh, Annie and John." I smiled at the thought of them but then frowned as another thought entered my mind. "You know, they might not be the only ones here. Janet did say there was another ghost who mostly prowled the grounds, but it wasn't that."

"You don't say."

I appreciated the way he tried to keep the sarcasm out of his voice this time.

CHAPTER 5

"Don't laugh, but last time I was here, I got the distinct impression that someone, or should I say some*thing* sinister, was creeping around." I hadn't actually seen anything, but I'd sure felt it.

"What do you mean?" Now I'd piqued his interest.

We were heading down the basement steps, the perfect setting for me to begin my spooky tale. Pete stopped at the bottom and waited for me to join him.

"Sure is gloomy down here." It surprised me when he suddenly took my hand and tucked it under his arm. "I don't want you to trip," he explained.

So, he was a gentleman. Very nice, I assured myself, not reading further into it.

There wasn't much to the basement. It consisted of three large rooms and a low ceiling that made Pete walk around with his head ducked. There was an ancient washer and dryer in one of the rooms, which appeared to be the only reason Janet would come down here. Well, that, and to add to her huge collection of preserves set on numerous shelves in one of the rooms. I'd seen a garden and an orchard from my window out back, which explained all the canned fruit and veggies. I guessed she hadn't gotten around to packing these up yet. Although, maybe she planned on leaving them behind. I believe she was heading into a retirement home, so space would no doubt be an issue.

Pete stopped before one of the shelves and examined some peaches. "So, you were saying?" he prompted me.

"Oh yeah, about something sinister.

Well, the story goes like this. John used to live in this house over a hundred years ago. Apparently, he was well respected and liked in the community. Since his dad died when he was about fifteen, and his mother was always ill, he took up the responsibility of caring for her and his three younger sisters. He left school and began to work at farming. At that time, the family owned about fifty acres here. Over the years, more and more were sold off."

"How much is left?" Pete tucked my hand, which had slipped down to my side, back under his arm as he began to lead me toward the stairway. I went along, figuring the poor guy's neck was probably killing him. I dislodged my hand and climbed the stairs.

"There are only about five acres now. Do you want to go outside?"

"Sure." We left the house and began a leisurely stroll toward the creek, where I took up telling the tale.

"John's mom passed away when John was about eighteen. He continued to farm the land and provide for his sisters until each one married and moved away. Then John found himself all alone in a big house."

"Sounds kinda lonely."

"I suppose he was for a while. Until he met Annie. She lived in town overtop a little bakery owned by her parents. John stopped in one day, and Annie was working behind the counter. Janet said she heard it was love at first sight."

"Sounds like an old cliché."

"I know. But it gets better, I promise."

"The pair dated and then got married and lived together here in this house. In the spring of nineteen-fourteen, when John was twenty-two, he went off to war, leaving Annie at home."

"I hope this isn't one of those stories about how the husband goes MIA, and the wife gets a letter and believes him to be dead, so she hooks up with another fella, and then the dead husband miraculously returns, finding his wife with the guy and then kills them and then himself in a jealous rage."

"No."

"Good."

"John was never declared missing in action, as far as I know. He did return home, but he wasn't alone. He brought a war buddy with him who he'd grown close to. The friend had no family, and John felt sorry for him. He needed help with the farm anyway. Annie hadn't been able to do much on her own, and the place needed to be brought up to snuff. So, all three of them lived here quite happily."

"Don't tell me. The friend falls for Annie, or she for him, and John kills them all in a jealous rage."

"No."

"Good."

"Can I continue, or would you like to come up with a few more jealous rage-killing scenarios?"

"No, I'm good."

I shook my head and concentrated on my story. "Anyway, the three of them lived here for about a year, and then one of John's sisters returned home, her marriage gone sour. John's friend took a liking to her, and John was happy about it, considering he'd never liked that particular brother-in-law. John told the pair they'd have his blessing to be together once his sister's divorce was finalized."

"So her jealous husband showed up and…."

"No!"

"Oh."

"The sister got her divorce and married the friend. John severed the land and gave them about ten acres and helped them build another house. That way, the two guys could help each other farm."

"That must be the place up the road where Janet's friend lives."

"Could be."

"It seems that John and Annie had a nice life here. Maybe that's why they decided to hang around after they died. Let me guess, John died an old man of ninety, and Annie soon followed after?"

"No, unfortunately, about six months after John's sister and his new brother-in-law moved into their newly built home, someone crept into John's house in the middle of the night and murdered him and Annie."

That declaration made Pete thoughtful. At least momentarily.

"Murdered? Did they ever catch who did it?" Pete asked.

"Nobody knows. They were stabbed to death. John was killed in the front foyer, but they found his body at the top of the stairs. Annie was killed in their bedroom. John left a trail of blood through the house, trying to get to her. He never made it."

"God, that's terrible."

"John's buddy — I think his name was Will — was also found dead, but it was back here." I motioned to the creek.

"So, the killer got him too?"

"That's the strange part. He was found face down, and when they rolled him over, they found the murder weapon in his belly."

"So, he was either running from the scene and tripped, landing on the knife, or he could have been chasing whoever it was who killed John and Annie," Pete said.

"That's the mystery they all took to their graves. With forensics being practically non-existent back then, the authorities didn't have much to go on. Although, they were able to dust for fingerprints. Nothing unusual was found, so the killer must have been wearing gloves, or it was someone known to frequent the house."

"Tragic."

"Yes, it was. John and Annie's chance at a life together was cut short. They never even got to have children."

Pete regarded me curiously for a moment, appearing hesitant to speak.

"What?" I finally asked.

"Can't you, you know?" There went those wiggling fingers of his again.

"You mean, can I talk to them and ask what happened?" I helped him along.

"Yeah."

I sighed. "That was my intention the last time I was here. After Janet told me the story, I was anxious to see them. Unfortunately, they didn't put in an appearance. Sure, they banged doors and creaked floors just to let us know they were around. But I didn't actually see them or the ghost that was giving off the creepy vibes, either. Maybe I will this time around."

The tour was now complete, and we strolled back to the house. We went into the kitchen, where Pete helped himself to more milk and cookies, and I prepared the chicken and popped it in the oven. I set the timer for an hour. "Okay, I'll add some carrots and potatoes when the timer goes off."

"Sounds good. So, after we eat, you want to go to bed, right?"

I stared at him stupidly.

"So we can get up at midnight?" He prompted.

"Yeah, right." What was the matter with me? Why was I acting like such a lovesick schoolgirl all of a sudden? I usually wasn't like this. But he was just so darn cute.

Despite being the auditor from hell.

CHAPTER 6

We spent the next hour fiddling around with my equipment. Pete wanted to see everything and know how to work it. He seemed genuinely interested, and not just because he was assessing my write-offs.

The timer went off while I was demonstrating my EVP machine. I hurried into the kitchen, peeled and diced two potatoes and two carrots and added them to the pot before setting the timer again. When I went back into the sitting room, Pete was sitting on the floor where I'd left him. The look on his face was shocked.

"Did you do this?" He waved the hand-held tape recorder before my face as I sat down with him.

"What?"

He fiddled with the buttons for a second and then handed the tape recorder to me. "Hit play."

I did, and then heard a static voice say, *John! John! I'm here.* The voice was female.

Pete was staring at me intently. "Did you do that? Or was it there before?"

"The tape is new. You saw me unwrap it and put it in. I always use a fresh tape for every job. Were you recording after I left the room?"

He hesitated a moment before he replied. "It's possible I could have hit the record button. So, do you think I caught that?"

"Yeah. It must have been Annie. Maybe she came in here after I went to the kitchen."

"Is she here now?" He looked about ready to bolt.

I swept my gaze around the room.

"No. I'd see her if she was. For some reason, they're avoiding me. Like they know I can see them."

"Let's do it again. Hit record, and we'll see if she talks some more." For someone who appeared so rattled, he seemed eager to continue.

"Okay. I don't want to lose that part with her talking already, so I'll start recording after that." I set up the machine how I wanted it.

"Be very quiet, all right? I'm going to ask some questions and see if I can get her to talk."

Pete looked to be holding his breath, so I began. "Annie? Are you here with us?" I paused and glanced around for any sign of her. If she didn't want me to see her, she could easily hide her ghostly form in the wall, or the furniture, which would still allow her to observe us and also answer my questions if she were so inclined.

Detecting a slight shadow lurking

behind a thick, cushy chair across the room, I continued. "Annie, don't be afraid. I can help you. We only want to talk."

"Is she here?" Pete whispered.

"Shhh," I directed at him, then turned back to stare at the chair. "Annie, please come out." With painstaking slowness, Annie finally crept from her hiding place and drifted over toward us. I handed the tape recorder to Pete and stood up to face her.

"What's happening?" Pete hissed.

"It's okay. She's here. Just sit quietly." Annie's presence was so faint I could clearly see the room right through her. "Annie, I'm Phoebe, and that's Pete. Can you tell me why you're so afraid? You're not scared of us, are you?"

"How can you see me?" Her gaze was distrustful as she looked back and forth from me to Pete.

"It's a gift I have. I was born with it."

"I'm dead," Annie said. "I was

murdered here in this house. A long time ago, I think."

"Yes. The year is twenty-twenty-three."

She gasped, clearly not expecting my reply. "The future. But still, the house stands. Thank God. What would happen to us if the house were gone?"

"Us? Do you mean you and John? Is there anyone else here?"

Her eyes darted around the room as she fidgeted. "I can't find John. Have you seen him?"

"No, I haven't."

"I've seen Will, but I can't find John." The way she mentioned Will didn't sound like she was frightened of him.

"Do you remember the night you were murdered? Do you know who did this to you and John?"

"And Will. He was killed too. It all happened so fast. I don't want to remember. It's too painful." She started to drift away. "I must find John."

"Annie, wait…." Too late, she was gone. I sat back down with Pete and gently pried the tape recorder from his hands. I switched it off and rewound the tape. When I hit play, I could clearly hear my voice talking to Annie, and faintly, in the background, I could hear Annie's replies.

"She was really here. You were really talking to her." He wore a goofy look on his face, and he was white as a sheet.

"And now I'm even more confused over this whole thing. I thought for sure that Will was the one who'd killed them. But now, I don't know."

A movement across the room suddenly caught my eye. A blur, quick as a flash, streamed over the floor and barreled right toward us, not stopping until it flew into Pete. Pete closed his eyes and put his hands to his head. He swayed for a moment.

"Pete. Are you okay?" What the hell was that? I'd never seen anything like it in my life.

Pete shook his head and opened his eyes. He stared at me as though he'd never seen me before. "My name is John," he said. "Why are you calling me Pete?"

There was no time for me to react. I heard a woman's voice—Annie, I think—yell, "John!" And then I caught the sight of another rapid flash across the room, this time bolting right into me.

Dizziness overcame me for a moment or two until finally, my head cleared, and—at long last—I looked into the eyes of the man I loved.

CHAPTER 7

"Annie, my love, my life!" John said, taking me into his arms.

Strange. I was still me, Phoebe, and yet I was also Annie at the same time. As though we'd become one, sharing our thoughts, our memories, our hopes, and our dreams, along with the same body. Pete must have had the same thing happen to him. John must have overtaken him. It was bizarre. I felt so overwhelmingly happy. It must be Annie who was feeling that.

John's lips came down on mine, his kiss making my toes curl in delight. It seemed like forever since I'd been in his arms. His hands were everywhere, exploring, awakening my every sense. I held him tight, my arms aching to hold him even closer.

Though I longed for his kiss to continue, I had to have answers. I pulled away. "John, where have you been? What happened to you?"

"I tried to reach you. I was so weak, so tired. So much blood," he said between kisses.

"Will? Have you seen him? He is here in the house too." This got his attention; he stopped abruptly and stood up. He walked toward the window and gazed outside for a while. When he turned back to me, I could see the anger in his face. It greatly confused me.

"That bastard! He betrayed me. He betrayed us all, Annie."

The rage in his voice and what he said made me jump to my feet. "You're wrong, John! I've spoken to Will. He was killed as well."

"Probably killed himself in shame,"

he sneered. "Do not be fooled by him any longer. I caught him downstairs with the knife in his hand. Covered in your blood." His voice broke.

"But, he is our friend. Married to your sister…."

"Yes. He made fools of us all."

"Why? What had he to gain from it?"

John shook his head. "I don't know. Greed perhaps? Wanted all the land, his farm and this one as well?"

"No. I don't believe it."

John came over and took me into his arms again. "He killed me, Annie. I saw him trying to escape the house with the knife. I charged at him, and when he turned around, he plunged the knife into me. He killed me just as he had you."

"No!" Annie couldn't handle the pain his words caused her. I felt myself get control back over my body as she let down her guard. Finally, she slipped away, leaving me like a shadow drifting past, and as she rushed from the room, I fell to the floor.

"No," John yelled. Then he, too, slipped from his host and rushed away. Pete soon joined me on the rug in a heap.

It took a moment or two for my head to clear. When I sat up and focused my sight, I saw Pete sitting up and looking around the room, stunned.

"What the hell was that?" he demanded, getting to his feet on unsteady legs. Though he glared daggers at me as though this was my fault, he at least offered me his hand in rising.

When I faced him, I said, "I'm sorry. That's never happened to me before." And it hadn't, although I couldn't deny I'd enjoyed kissing John — or Pete — and I know Annie had been all for it.

"It was me, but at the same time, it wasn't me."

"I felt the same way. Annie was doing all the driving, and I was along for the ride. Like a captive audience." I could feel my face heat up a little when I realized what I just said. "I mean…."

"I know what you mean," Pete interrupted.

"Are you upset?" Before he could answer me, the timer in the kitchen went off.

"The chicken's done." He strode off without answering my question.

We ate in silence. From the look on his face, I could see he had a battle waging inside of him. It wasn't every day you realized ghosts were real. And it was even rarer still when one possessed you.

"Are you okay?" I finally asked him as I got up to scrape off my plate into the garbage and put it into the sink. "Do you still want to go through with this, or have you changed your mind? I could always drive you back to town."

"And then what? Come back out here by yourself? No way." Did I detect a protective tone in his voice?

"It's not like it's the first time I've

done this, you know," I reminded him.

He rose and scraped his plate and put it in the sink with mine. I started running the water to wash up the few dirty dishes we'd made.

"You said it was the first time something like that had ever happened to you."

"True," I relented. "But it doesn't scare me. Not much does."

"Well, I'm not scared," Pete insisted.

Oh, dear. I'd gone and hurt his masculine pride. "I'm sure you're not."

"Maybe just a little freaked out." He picked up a tea towel and started to dry.

"I'm intrigued."

"About what?"

"This mystery. Annie was killed by someone, and everything pointed to Will, but why wouldn't she be afraid of him?"

He shrugged. "Do you think he's that dark presence you detected on your last visit?" So, he had been listening.

"I dunno. It's possible." I pondered for a moment. "Do you think maybe Annie doesn't know who killed her? After all, it was night, and she was stabbed in her bed. It could have been too dark."

"If she'd been asleep before it happened, it's possible she may not know."

"What if it was a prowler, and he got away? All this time, he could have been wandering the streets."

"There's a pleasant thought." The dishes done, Pete tossed his towel onto the drying rack. I pulled the drain plug and used his towel to dry my hands.

"Let's get some rest, and we'll resume this at midnight," I said.

We strolled up to the top of the stairs together. His bedroom was first, but he lingered by the doorway after I said 'goodnight.'

"Something wrong?" He wasn't scared again, was he?

"You don't think they'll do that again,

do you? While we're asleep?" He looked around the hall nervously as though he, too, could see the dead.

I swept my gaze around. "I don't see them lurking, but hey, anything's possible." *Let the nonbeliever chew on that while he lays in bed alone.*

Pete gave me a look crossed between annoyance and trepidation. Without another word, he went into his room and shut the door tight behind him. I strolled down the hall to my own room, grinning as I went. If anything, this should take care of my little audit problem.

Good.

CHAPTER 8

I awoke precisely at midnight. When I opened my door, Pete was leaning against the wall opposite my room. It looked like he hadn't slept a wink.

"How 'bout I make a big pot of coffee before we head up?" He wasn't going to be much help to me, the condition he was in. Probably used to getting a solid eight hours a night. Ah, the perks of a day job.

Twenty minutes later, we were hunkered down in the attic. I'd checked the camera, and nothing had recorded yet.

"So, what do we do?" Pete whispered. He sat next to me on an old loveseat pushed against the wall. The only remaining furniture in the huge space.

"We wait."

From the way his gaze kept darting around the room, I knew he was nervous about the possession fiasco. It'd shaken me up as well. The intensity of having another soul in my body, feeling what she felt, having emotions course though me that weren't my own, was completely foreign to me. Pete shuddered, and although I suspected it was from fear, not cold, the attic did seem a bit drafty.

After we sat in silence for a few minutes, he asked, "How long does something like this usually take?"

"Depends," I answered.

"You don't think they'll, you know, jump us again, do you?"

I shrugged. Geesh, had kissing me been *that* terrible? Pete was keeping his eyes on the camera closest to us. Presented with his handsome profile, I studied him. "What made you become an auditor?"

He turned his gaze back to me, a puzzled expression on his face. Now it was his turn to shrug. "The excitement, I suppose." He was completely serious.

"Really?"

"Yeah. I like to dig into people's files like a private investigator, searching for clues. And the ones that cheat—bringing them down gives me huge satisfaction."

When I remembered the entire reason for him being here with me now was to *bring me down*, I frowned at him. "Not everyone is trying to get away with something."

He took my hand suddenly, which surprised me. "Phoebe, look, I know I came out here with you hoping to write this whole thing off as a joke, but I gotta tell you, I believe you."

He appeared sincere enough. "Really?"

"Yes. And when we get back, I'm going to recommend you be allowed your write-offs as legitimate business expenditures."

"Wow. Thanks," I said.

"I have to say, you've opened my eyes to things I'd never considered before."

"Like ghosts?"

He chuckled a little as though he couldn't believe it himself. "Yes, like ghosts."

Then he was leaning toward me on that tiny uncomfortable couch, and his lips brushed gently against mine. My arms, seeming to have a mind of their own, reached up to slide around his neck and pulled him closer. *What are you doing?* A voice warned me, yet soon I was leaning back on the couch, and Pete was practically overtop of me, his lips still locked onto mine and his arms wrapped tight around me.

A sudden crash made us break apart, and we jumped to our feet. "What was that?" I demanded, my heart beating frantically.

"I don't know, you're the ghost buster."

To my dismay, my camera, the other one across the room, was lying in three pieces on the floor. "What the hell?" I stalked toward it, but before I made it to the camera, the attic door flung open so hard it hit the wall. Pete couldn't see the apparition standing there, tall and overbearing, but I could.

"What do you want?" I tried to appear brave, but my voice came out in a squeak.

"Who are you talking to?" Pete asked. "Is someone there?"

"You must leave this place!" the specter demanded. "You will ruin everything." Our presence obviously agitated him. I wasn't sure why.

"Are you Will?" It must be him, it wasn't John. I knew John since we'd been intimately introduced.

The ghost seemed taken aback. "How do you know my name?"

"I've seen Annie. She said you were here in the house with her." Though he was angry and upset, he didn't seem menacing. Mostly he was scared, I think.

"Who are you talking to?" Pete repeated.

I looked over my shoulder and saw him frozen to the spot. Ignoring him, I concentrated on Will. It was the first time I'd seen him, and I didn't want to blow this chance. "I've seen John too." I watched for a reaction. I knew Annie didn't blame Will for her and John's deaths, but I knew that John did.

The ghost visibly recoiled. He looked around as though frightened. "John was here? In the house?"

"Yes. He's angry with you. He said you killed him."

He appeared to ponder my statement before he responded. "I…did kill him. I didn't mean to do it."

"It was an accident? Did you kill Annie by accident too?" That question seemed to make him mad.

When he spoke, it was loudly and with conviction. "Yes. I killed them. Both of them."

"Are you sure about that?" Something didn't seem quite right. He appeared to be trying to convince himself, not just me.

"No. I mean, yes. I'm guilty. I killed them. If you see them, John and Annie, tell them they can be together. Tell them to go, to move on, or whatever it is we're supposed to do."

"Why do you think they haven't moved on yet?"

"I've seen Annie," he admitted. "She said she couldn't find John. But if you've seen them both, then they're together now. They can leave."

"What about you?"

"Doesn't matter what happens to me. I can wait."

Before I could say another word, Will suddenly vanished. I looked over at Pete, who was watching me intently. "He's gone," I told him.

"What'd he say? I only got half the

conversation."

My poor camera lay in pieces at my feet. I knelt down to examine the damage and spoke to Pete over my shoulder. "He admits to killing both Annie and John."

"It's what everyone suspected, right?" Pete came over to get a closer look as I tried to reassemble the parts of my camera. It wasn't broken, only in pieces.

"I don't know. Something didn't seem right about the way he acted. It was as though he was trying hard to make me believe he was guilty."

"But you're not convinced?" He helped me adjust the tripod, then after I got up, we reattached the camera to it.

I made a few adjustments, checking the focus and that the tape was set to record. "I don't know. He seemed pretty adamant for Annie and John move along to the afterworld now that they're together."

"Maybe he's tired of keeping out of John's way?" Pete surmised.

"Possibly. Although I'm not sure it's going to be easy to get John and Annie to move on. I mean, after all this time, they finally meet again, and it's only because they overtake our bodies. What's kept them apart until now?"

"I dunno. You said they found John's body trying to get to Annie, and he didn't make it."

"Yeah. But what's he been doing over the years? Searching for Will to get his revenge?"

"Unresolved issues. That's why ghosts don't cross over, isn't it?"

I smirked at him. He didn't seem as obtuse about the afterlife as he pretended to be. "It's mostly the reason why."

"You'd think if he was so desperate to get to Annie, then that would be his priority. Not going after Will."

"Unless something was keeping him from her," I mused.

"Something like what?"

"His guilt."

Chapter 9

We sat back down on the couch and reached for our coffee cups. The kiss we'd shared earlier was all but forgotten in the excitement of Will's unexpected visit.

"You think John feels guilty that he couldn't save Annie?"

"Sure, he must. He probably feels he failed to protect her, and he couldn't bring himself to face her."

"You would think after all John did for him, Will would feel bad about killing them. Maybe Will regretted it so much that he took his own life?"

"Yeah, but he still sees Annie. If he felt so bad for killing them, why would he make himself known to her?" I questioned. Mysteries weren't really my forte.

"Maybe Will is trying to get Annie to intercede with John for him?" Pete pondered.

"But Annie didn't say anything like that to me. She knew she was killed, but she doesn't suspect Will."

"He's a good actor then?"

I put my cup aside and got up from the couch. "Well, sitting here isn't going to give us the answers. I think we need to go on a little ghost hunt."

Pete climbed to his feet. Though he looked less than enthused with my idea, he said, "Lead on Macduff," and gestured toward the door.

As we walked through the house — me on hot alert for any ghostly presences — I thought about Will again. "Do you think someone else could have killed Annie? Maybe Will heard her screams and rushed to her rescue but arrived too late? And before you say it, I mean if somehow John didn't hear her screams. Maybe he was partially deaf from the war, or a deep sleeper, or outside doing whatever?"

"Okay, so if Will heard screams, rushed over, and happened to find the murder weapon, and John caught him with the knife…."

"Exactly. Then John and Will may have quarreled, and it could be, as Will said, that he killed John by accident."

"Then Will could have rushed from the house attempting to find the real killer, or maybe even go for help, but then either slipped and impaled himself on the knife or else he did find the killer, and he was murdered as well."

"Sure, it could have happened that way. But then, why take the blame for killing them both?" I asked. "Do you think Will may have felt so overwrought about killing John and letting the killer get away that he just decided to say he killed both Annie and John?"

"Perhaps. It's an interesting theory," Pete agreed.

"All this time. All this misguided guilt."

We were halfway down the staircase when I saw a sudden streak of light flash from the sitting room into the kitchen. I hurried down the last few steps and bolted in the same direction, Pete hot on my heels. When I reached the kitchen. I could see Annie standing by the sink. She must have heard our advance. She turned and stared at me in fright.

"Don't be afraid, Annie," I said.

Pete snorted.

Ignoring him, I walked toward Annie with my hands up in a placating manner. "I've just spoken to Will," I told her.

"Have you seen John? I can't find him," Annie said. "He was here, and then he was gone."

"I think he's looking for Will."

"He said Will killed us. I don't believe

it. Will loved us, all of us. Especially John's sister. We were all so happy. He never would have done anything to jeopardize that. I don't know what happened."

"Can you remember anything about the night you died?" I could see by her expression she didn't want to remember. "I know it's hard, Annie. But you need to try."

I felt a shiver of cold air surround me. "Leave her alone," said a voice from the shadows.

A moment later, John stepped forward, and Annie and I both said in surprise, "John!"

"Oh no! Where?" demanded Pete.

"Shush!" I hissed at him.

John floated over to Annie and took her into his arms. "My love," he said.

"Oh, John, John," Annie gushed.

It seemed they had finally reconnected. Thankfully, without our help this time. "You can move on now," I told them.

"I can't," John said. "Not until I've

dealt with Will."

"You're dead. Forget about vengeance. What has it done for you all these years except keep you from the woman you love?"

John glared at me, and I took an involuntary step backward. "How can I let him get away with what he did? You think I can just move on and let Will go free?"

"He isn't free. He's eaten up with guilt and remorse. He'll probably spend the rest of eternity haunting this house living with what he's done." Well, not really *living* with it. Not to mention this place was about to get a lot worse when the 'haunted B&B' opened for business. At least if one ghost was still around, I guess I wouldn't have to worry about a lawsuit.

"No. I'm sorry, Annie," he said, gazing into the face of the woman he loved. Then he vanished.

Annie cried out in sorrow, then she was gone too.

"Well, that went well," I said.

"Are they gone?" Pete asked, coming up to stand beside me.

"Yes. And John refuses to leave without confronting Will."

"And let me guess, Annie refuses to leave without John?"

"Looks like we're back to square one."

We sat in the sitting room for another half-hour before I decided to call it a night. Pete had yawned loudly ever since we sat down, and I didn't think the trio was going to put in another appearance.

"Let's go to bed." Pete nodded in agreement. We walked upstairs, and I stopped at his door. "Try to get some sleep."

"I should walk you to your room," he said, trying to be gallant.

"It's okay. You're not used to all this late-night excitement. I'll be fine." I could see he was exhausted. "Goodnight." Before I could turn away, he reached out and snatched my hand. He pulled me toward him and kissed me.

"Goodnight," he said. He let go of my hand and went into his room. The door shut, and I stared at it stupidly for a moment before shaking my head. Smiling, I walked down the hall to my own room.

~*~

The smell of coffee woke me the next morning. I reached for my watch on the bedside table and saw it was just after nine. Pete was sitting at the kitchen table when I walked in. His arms were stretched out in front of him, resting on the table. He held a mug in both hands and was staring off into space.

"Morning," I spoke softly so I didn't startle him.

Blinking a few times, he refocused his gaze on me and smiled tightly. "Hey."

"Sleep okay?" I grabbed a mug out of the cupboard and poured myself some coffee that looked like it'd been made a while ago.

"Yeah, sure," he said. "You?"

I added some milk from the fridge to my cup, then pulled out the chair across from him and sat down. "Yes, thanks." Adding sugar, I stirred my coffee and took a sip. Yep, definitely old.

"Nothing else happen?" His voice was indifferent, but I guessed he was quite interested in my answer.

"Nope," I didn't elaborate. There was nothing to tell.

He let go of his mug and ran a hand over his face. "Want to head into town and have breakfast? My treat."

I shrugged. "Okay, if you like." He was probably anxious to get out of here. I was tempted to offer to drive him home again, but I didn't want to offend him. Not when he'd said he believed in what I did. I also had selfish reasons for not wanting to let him go. At least until I'd reaffirmed my write-offs as being legitimate and maybe figured out what that kiss we'd shared was all about.

Town wasn't far, so we decided to walk. It was a beautiful clear day, with hardly a cloud in the sky.

Last time I was here, I'd driven through downtown just to pop into the gas station to top up the tank and grab some snacks for the ride home. Other than that, I'd never been here before. The town was named Emerald. Probably because most of the year it was nestled on all sides by vast green forest. Population, according to the big wooden sign, was just under five thousand. It being late October, a smattering of leaves had begun to fall, decorating surfaces with a riot of color. The air was fresh and crisp, and pumpkins and Halloween décor graced every home we saw.

Small towns were great. I remembered my Granny watching a show that had a town named Mayberry. Everyone knew each other, and everyone waved and gossiped and knew each else's business. It had to be weird living like that. Having always been in a big city, I barely knew a handful of my neighbors in the same building I lived in.

Stealing a glance at Pete, walking tall beside me, hands stuffed into the pockets of his fall jacket, I sensed the tension slipping away from him. Granted, it'd been a rough go of it for someone not used to my line of work. Even I, being used to the macabre, was feeling the effects.

We spotted a diner named *Jimmy's* and decided to eat there. A bell jangled when Pete opened the door, and he gestured me inside. A booth by the window looked inviting, so I slid into a seat, Pete taking the one across from me. The waitress, a woman in her fifties with a smile as big as her bosom, placed menus on the table.

"New in town?" she asked, whipping out her pad and pencil, her kindly eyes appraising Pete and giving me an approving wink.

"Yes," I answered. Pete nodded, his attention focused on the menu.

"Business or pleasure?" she asked.

"Um, business." I didn't want a lot of people knowing what I was doing here, so I didn't elaborate. Her nametag said, *Grace*. I wondered if she was related to Jimmy.

Grace gazed at Pete again before returning her attention to me. "Shame."

Pete cleared his throat and proceeded to order the meat lover's special, along with three eggs, toast, and home fries. Obviously, he wasn't too freaked out to lose his appetite.

"I'll just have three slices of bacon, toast, and one egg, please," I said, reaching for Pete's menu and passing them back to her. "And coffee."

"Sure thing, sweetie," Grace said, winking at me again and sidling off. She brought us over two mugs of black coffee with a dish of creamers and sugar packs.

I stirred in two sugars and two creamers and sipped. Much better than the coffee I'd had this morning. Most likely, that had more to do with its age than the person who made it.

About ten minutes later, our breakfast arrived. Pete had his nose buried in today's paper and continued to read while he ate. I sighed and dug into my food. He hadn't said a word to me since we sat down. Whether that boded well for me personally or professionally, I had no idea. Halfway through our meal, the door jangled again, and I saw Janet walk in with a woman of similar age. Her friend, no doubt. When Janet looked in our direction, I waved, and she smiled and nudged her companion. Both strolled over to stand at our table.

"How nice to see you, Phoebe," Janet said. "Lara, this is the young woman I told you about, and her young man, Pete, isn't it?" she directed that part at Pete, who observed the pair over his periodical. He folded up the paper and smiled.

"Yes, it's Pete," he affirmed.

"We're only half-way though breakfast," I said. "Would you like to join us?" If this was the woman who lived in the house of John's sister and Will, then I really wanted to talk to her and see if she could offer any info on the couple.

Janet looked at Lara, and the woman nodded. "That would be lovely," Janet said. Pete and I slid over, making room for the two women. Janet sat beside me. Lara blushed a little as she slid in next to Pete. I eyed Lara, wondering how much she knew about me and my line of work.

Grace came over and placed two menus on the table. Lara thanked her and picked one up. "I'm not very hungry this morning," she said to no one in particular. Then, she peered at me. "How was your first night in the haunted house?" she asked with a smile.

I returned her smile. "Quite unexpected," I admitted.

"Oh, you're the ghost hunter girl!" Grace boomed.

Now everyone in the diner stared at

me.

So much for flying under the radar.

CHAPTER 10

At least the diner wasn't overly crowded. Although, I guess it didn't matter much since word would no doubt spread fast.

Small towns.

Lara must have noticed the hush that suddenly came over the place. She peered around with a guilty look on her face. Grace didn't seem aware, or didn't care, about our table being under scrutiny. She had me pinned to my seat with her bulging eyeballs, waiting for a reply to her question.

"Um, yeah, I guess you could call me that," I admitted.

Grace clapped her hands together like she was squashing a flying insect.

"Marvelous! About time somebody got down to figuring out what's going on in that house."

Janet tossed a cool glance Grace's way, which had an immediate effect.

"I'll grab the coffee pot and another pair of cups," Grace mumbled as she scrambled away.

Janet eyed the others in the diner with a pointed stare, and they all quickly became enamored with their plates. Now, if I'd had that effect on people, I wouldn't be stuck in this predicament of proving myself to Pete.

And yet, I had to admit, as I perused his fine form, I wasn't feeling as put out as I should be.

"Go on, dear," Lara urged. "You were telling us about your night."

I waited until Grace slunk over and set down two cups, and poured the coffee in record time before speeding off.

"Um, it was pretty active." When Pete snorted, I shot him a look.

"Oh, dear," Janet said. "I've noticed they seemed rather upset since the For Sale sign went up. Though it's probably unlikely, I have a feeling that deep down they sense a change coming."

Lara nodded her head resolutely. "Yep, I do believe ghosts have ESP or some such connection to the netherworld that allows them to know things."

"Do you really think so?" Janet lifted her cup and sipped, her hands visibly trembling.

"Are you all right?" I asked her.

She set down her coffee and smiled at me. "Yes, yes, dear. I'm fine. I just can't help but feel responsible for the unrest in my house."

"Not your house much longer," Lara reminded her, not unkindly.

Janet sighed. "Do they seem willing to move on? I can't stand the thought of them being used by that man for entertainment and profit."

I was tempted to ask Pete if there were any taxable reasons the venture couldn't be allowed, but when I looked at him, I noticed he'd sunk deeper into his seat and pulled the paper up to hide his face again. I frowned.

"Last night, I made contact and tried to reason with them," I told the pair, who stared at me avidly. "They appeared caught up in the drama of their lives—I mean, the lives they had." I turned my attention to Lara. "Is your house the one that John's sister lived in with Will?"

Lara nodded. "Yes, it is, but there are no ghosts there. At least, none that I've ever seen."

"Yes," agreed Janet. "They seem to all be at my property where the deaths took place."

"Okay, so John's sister isn't still there waiting for Will to return?" I clarified.

"Not as far as I know," Lara confirmed. "Besides, she remarried a little over a year later and had three kids."

"How do you know?" I asked.

"Because one of the kids is my dad. He inherited the house from his mom — my grandmother — and he and my mother lived there and had three more kids. I have two older brothers. I bought them out of the house when my parents passed away. I've lived there since I was a child."

"Yes, we grew up together," Janet clarified. "I've lived at my house all my life."

I knew Janet was a widow with no children. She told me during our first meeting. The ghosts had been present all her life. When she was very little, she'd told me she recalled being able to see them, but over time, she lost that ability. Over the years, she'd continued to have things happen, but her parents hadn't believed in such nonsense, so Janet had kept her encounters to herself.

"Janet, have you ever met anyone else on the property besides John, Annie and Will?" I was sure I'd felt something else.

Something lurking in the shadows, hiding, and watching.

She appeared thoughtful of my question. "No. Not that I recall. It's always just been the three of them. Why? Did you see something else...someone else?"

"I'm sure it was nothing," I was quick to assure her. "I did notice the trio are wrapped up in their drama. Annie seems to have no clue as to how or why she was killed. John and Will are at odds with one another. John blames Will for their deaths. And Will is more than happy to take responsibility for what happened, but I think he's innocent."

"Do you really?" Lara asked. "There were always rumors around town that my grandmother's first husband had been in love with Annie and that one night he'd killed her and John in a jealous rage. Then killed himself out of guilt. I always felt bad for my grandmother.

"There's a lot more going on than what we or even the ghosts know," I said.

"I just need to get to the bottom of it before there's any chance of them moving on."

"Oh, dear. I think this may take longer than a couple of days," Janet said. "Do you need more time, Phoebe?"

I shrugged. "I might."

"You're more than welcome to stay with me as long as you need to," Lara told Janet.

"Thank you, that's very kind," Janet said. "Can you stay? Until it's done, then?" she asked me.

The look on her face, a mixture of hope and fearful anxiety, made me nod my head. "Yes, I can stay." Then I remembered I wasn't alone in this venture.

As if he felt our scrutiny, Pete slowly lowered his paper.

"If you need to return, I can drive you home and come back here," I offered.

"There's a bus that runs out to the city from here, I'm sure," Janet said helpfully.

Pete stared at me. "No. I have my

laptop and can work remotely if I need to. Plus, I have some vacation time coming to me, and I can't think of any other place I'd rather spend it," he surprised me by saying. "I want to see this through till the end."

Lara beamed at us both. "Then it's all settled."

"Yes, it appears so," Janet said while Pete and I silently exchanged a glance.

~*~

Since we were staying longer, Pete and I decided to stroll through town and pick up a few items. We'd left Janet and Lara at the diner finishing their breakfast.

We settled on a pharmacy slash general store. They even had some clothing in there—mostly sweatshirts with silly logos or track pants for tourists. Since it was the end of the summer season, and the fall and winter season was in full swing, the prices were outrageous.

Pete came over to the rack of apparel where I stood, eyeing the price of a T-shirt.

"What's the matter?" he asked, noting the disapproval on my face.

"These prices," I hissed, keeping my voice down so the shop employee wouldn't overhear. Even the summer items were overpriced.

Pete checked out a few of the garments and raised an eyebrow. "Pick out whatever you like. I'll pay," he offered.

"You can't do that," I objected.

He pulled a sweatshirt off the rack and held it up to me. "Sure, I can. Don't worry, I'll just write it off."

Of course, he would. He worked as an auditor. For the government. He probably wrote off half the stuff in his life.

Though I didn't like it, I settled on a few clothing and personal items and let Pete purchase everything along with his own stuff. Outside I couldn't help but comment on the broad smile on his face.

"What's got you so thrilled?"

He shrugged. "Nothing like a little

retail therapy." Seeing my frowny face, he went on, "The sun is shining. I'm in a cozy town for Halloween, not stuck inside staring at four walls crunching numbers."

And not ruining lives, I wanted to add. But then, a thought struck me. Something he'd said that had completely slipped my mind. Halloween was just days away. And I was not only going to spend it in a sleepy little hollow but in an actual haunted house with a government auditor.

A handsome one.

I wasn't sure which of these things was more terrifying.

CHAPTER 11

When we returned to the house, there was a car in the driveway I didn't recognize.

"That's not Lara's car," Pete noted.

"No, it's not," I agreed as the driver of the vehicle climbed out of the front seat and waited for us to come closer.

"Friend of yours?" Pete asked quietly as we both stared at the tall, heavyset man whose gaze seemed to be taking stock of us. Under such scrutiny, I couldn't help but feel uneasy and lacking.

"Ah, so it appears to be true," the man said as we came up before him and stopped.

"Excuse me?" I ventured.

Dramatically, he gestured toward

the driver's side of my jeep, which sported decals of little ghosts fleeing a net and the words *I'm the one to call*. An advertisement for my business I'd listed as a write-off.

"Hey, that's cute. I didn't notice that before," Pete said.

"I don't think it's cute at all," the man snapped. "I know who you are," he held out his cell phone, which displayed my website—another right off.

Pete looked at me and shrugged. "Well, that makes one of us."

"I'm Henry Costa," the man said as though that should suffice as an answer.

Then I remembered a conversation I'd had with Janet. *Oh oh.*

"Oh, hi. Nice to meet you."

"Wish I could say the same," Henry said.

Just when I could see that Pete had quite enough of Mr. Costa's rudeness, I placed a hand on his arm to stop what I was sure was going to be a tirade.

"Um, Pete, this is the buyer, you know, of Janet's house?" I watched his face as he put it together.

"Oh yes, the haunted B&B," Pete said sarcastically.

"Exactly," Henry exclaimed. "The key component being *haunted*. When I purchased this property, it was precisely for the reason of it being haunted. Now I must warn you, I will be forced to take legal action against you and the previous owner if I should find my property no longer in the state in which I had purchased it."

Pete actually laughed. "I'd love to see that one stand up in court, buddy."

The fact Pete found this amusing calmed me somewhat. But Henry's face began to take on the shade of a boiled lobster.

"I...will...sue," he sputtered.

"Mr. Costa, I assure you the house is still very much haunted," I said before Pete could respond. By the way his ham-sized fists were squeezing, I could tell he was furious. The last thing we needed was a battle.

My words appeared to have the desired effect on Mr. Costa. His face lightened two shades, and his glare softened somewhat.

"At least for now, it is," Pete said, wiping away all the progress I'd made.

"What is that supposed to mean?" Henry said with a snarl.

Pete took a step toward him, and Henry, smaller in size, stepped back.

"It means Phoebe and I are going to do what we set out to do."

"Which is?" Henry said, though he probably already knew the answer.

"Cross these ghosts over. And maybe we'll even have a good cry at the end as well."

Oh, for f—

"I'm warning you, when I take possession of my property on the first of November, if I fail to find it in the condition of which I purchased it—haunted—then I intend to sue. All of you!"

Before another word was spoken, Henry practically dove into the front seat of his car, slammed the door, and sped off down the driveway leaving Pete and I standing there with our mouths hanging open.

"Oh boy," I said.

Pete reached out and took my hand, the one not holding a bag full of government write-offs. "Relax. Don't give him a second thought."

"But you heard what he said. He's gonna sue me and Janet too if I cross over the ghosts."

"I'm surprised at you." He led me to the porch and up the steps.

"Why's that?" He took the bag from my hand so I could find the key and unlock the door.

"You face off ghosts for a living. The undead. And you're scared of that joker?"

He held open the door as I went inside, then followed me.

He had a point.

"I don't like the idea of being sued." *Or audited*, for that matter, I didn't add. We took off our jackets and shoes and headed into the kitchen. I knew I had an issue of being a people pleaser. But I hated being disliked by anyone, regardless if they warranted my consideration or not. My mom had tried to drum it into my head over countless years that not everyone I met was going to like me, and that was *okay*. Sometimes I feared I went to extremes by isolating myself— living alone, working alone, working with the dead, for God's sake—just so I wouldn't have to come across anyone I wouldn't jive with. And I admit, upon occasion, I had a tendency to be stand-offish. Or downright cold, just to avoid getting close to anyone so they couldn't dislike me.

"People will believe what they want to believe. It's an old house. I'm sure even without the ghosts, it'll be plenty spooky."

"So, you want me to lie?" I clarified.

"No, not lie exactly."

"Then what?"

"Don't say anything at all. You don't have to admit anything to Henry Costa. You probably won't even see him again," Pete assured me.

The fact that he appeared to have every faith in my ability to cross over the trio of wayward ghosts comforted me somewhat.

"I can't leave Janet holding the bag. Even though she hired me to do the job, and I admit, I knew all the details of the buyer's plans for this house, I can't let her face him alone. You saw what a bully he is."

Pete snorted. Of course, he wouldn't find the man intimidating.

"How did he even know I was here?"

A couple beats later, we said in unison, "Small towns." *Of course.* One of his spies had probably been in the diner.

"Do you think he's staying in town?"

I wondered aloud.

Pete went to the fridge and took out a glass pitcher of lemonade. I grabbed a pair of glasses from the cupboard, and we sat down at the kitchen table.

"Possibly. If he's taking possession soon, he may be getting things ready for the B and B if he plans to open quickly."

"Yeah, he seemed anxious to get in here. I wonder if he's planning on staying here himself or if he's going to hire staff?"

"Maybe both. He might stick around for a bit till things get up and running."

"Yeah, and to make sure the ghosts are still here," I said.

That sinking feeling I had when I'd first decided to take this job began to resurface. Pete smiled at me, no doubt seeing the angst on my face. He reached across the table for my hand, and when I felt his warm, firm grip on mine, I felt better knowing I wasn't alone. And as scary as Costa had been, he didn't hold a candle to my auditor.

CHAPTER 12

The ghosts made an appearance right before lunch. Pete had whipped us up grilled cheese sandwiches, and we'd just sat down at the table to eat when the lemonade pitcher fell off the counter, shattering into a million pieces.

Pete jumped higher than I did.

"Holy crap, that scared me." I gave a little laugh despite the calamity and my heart galloping away in my chest. I noticed Pete was staring around, his hands spread out as though ready to wrestle someone. Both of us probably worried about the same thing—a repeat of that smoochie kiss we'd been forced to act out. No way was I going to let myself get possessed again. If I could help it, that was.

"Is there someone here?" he demanded.

Sweeping the room with my gaze, I shook my head. "Not that I can see." There'd been a shadowy streak that had flown out of the kitchen after the crash, but I hadn't had the chance to look at it closely. Now that the moment had passed, I stared at the mess on the floor.

"Damn, what do you want to bet that was Janet's favorite pitcher?" I asked.

Pete went to the tall cupboard to search for a broom. He came out with one, along with a dustpan, as I grabbed paper towels for the spill.

"Careful not to cut yourself," he instructed, seeing me dabbing at the lemonade on the floor among the broken glass.

Well, duh.... So much for thinking I could handle myself.

We cleaned up the mess, wrapping the shards of glass in newspaper before disposing of them in the trash. I made a mental note to grab a new pitcher in town the next time I went in, hoping I could find something similar. Returning the broom and dustpan to the cupboard, I stepped in and put them away while admiring the tidy space. It was a lot roomier than I thought it'd be. On the right side were some narrow shelves for cleaning supplies, and the left side had hooks to hang things. The back of the cupboard had a couple of shelves along with some hooks underneath. The bottom shelf, I noticed, was quite narrow and not very deep—at least, not enough to put something on without worrying it'd fall off. And it was also slightly on an angle, as though one of the nails had come loose. When I lifted the dipped right side, thinking perhaps I could fix it for Janet, the shelf made a clicking sound. It wiggled slightly, so I pushed a bit harder, attempting to lift it again, and felt around for a nail, or at least a hole that the nail would go in. But the spot was smooth against my finger. And then I noticed, because of the pushing I'd done, that the back of the wall seemed to move slightly.

"Oh no," I called out.

"What's the matter?"

"I dunno. I think I broke something." The space darkened when Pete moved into the doorway. "I was trying to straighten this little shelf at the back, but the whole wall seems to be coming loose now."

He stepped in, making the area almost claustrophobic. I wigged over to give him room as he examined the shelf. He made some tutting noises as he ran his fingers up and along the crevice I'd created.

"Interesting," he said.

"What? That I broke the wall? Janet isn't going to be thrilled that her pitcher is broken, and now her wall…."

"Ta-da." He pushed at the wall,

causing it to make a crunching sound followed by a groan.

"Oh wow! Is that a—"

"A door?" he interrupted. "Yes, it would appear so."

"Oh, cool," I gushed, staring into the dark depth. "I didn't know there were trap doors in this house." By the look of it, Janet hadn't either, considering the long dangling cobwebs and the thick layer of dust on the ground.

"You know we're going to have to explore this, right?"

"You're game?" I was only slightly surprised. I mean, who wouldn't want to explore a hidden passageway?

"Sure. We're going to need flashlights. And let's eat first." Always pragmatic. Though I had to admit he was right.

We ate quickly and even took the time to find another pitcher— this time using a plastic one—and made more lemonade to drink.

My gear included several excellent
flashlights, and we opted to use a large
one that could be carried or set down on its
base, which Pete offered to hold. I shoved
a penlight in my pocket and gave him one
as backup, and grabbed a practical cylinder
light with a beam that could be adjusted
in size. We also changed into hiking boots
that, thankfully, we'd both thought to pack
as 'just in case' apparel and put on light
jackets considering there was a slight breeze
coming from the trap door.

Prepared, we passed through the
cupboard and then went through the
doorway at the back. Pete wanted to go first,
but I'd argued he would block any view I'd
have, so he relented and let me go ahead of
him. Shining my light all around, I noted the
floor was old wide planks of hardwood, and
the walls appeared drywalled. They may
have been painted white or cream colored
at one time, but now they were so faded it
was hard to tell. They even peeled in some

places.

"Maybe we should have brought a broom along for all these cobwebs." I brushed more danglers out of the way with my flashlight.

"Yeah, it'd help in case of bats too."

I cringed. "I hadn't thought of that."

"It's not too late to go back," he said in a spooky voice.

I chuckled good naturedly and veered right as the passage led off that way. Overhead, I noted the space was about six feet high since Pete had to duck slightly. His broad shoulders just barely fit the narrow width.

"I wonder what this was used for?"

"Janet didn't mention it?"

"No. She didn't."

I stopped suddenly when I came to a crossroads. To my left, a narrow staircase wound up. To my right, the passageway slanted down. The area I stood in was wider than the passage area, and Pete came up beside me to contemplate our next move.

"Don't suggest we split up," he said, reading my mind.

"Okay, then, let's go this way." I indicated the slope to the right. "I have a feeling this either goes to the basement or outside."

When we reached the end of the line, there were almost a dozen rickety wooden steps to climb. At the top was a wooden door. From this side, I could smell the cool fresh air from outside. When I jiggled the handle, I heard a click, and I pushed. Pete reached over my shoulder and aided my action. With his help, I opened the door, which probably had remained immobile for decades, and we stepped into another space.

Dimming daylight streamed through the pair of little windows. We turned off our flashlights.

"Where are we?"

"I'm not sure," I admitted. Everything was covered in dust. There was an array of tools hanging on hooks and nails on a wall over where a table had been placed. There were planters and other containers on the table, along with a few more gardening tools. Against another wall leaned rakes and shovels and a hoe.

"Appears to be a shed." The exit door was directly across from us. I looked around Pete at the door we'd come through. He turned to look as well. Closing that door, I moved beside him.

"From here, it just looks like a closet," I noted.

Pete nodded in agreement. "Let's go outside and see where we are."

"Okay." I let him take the lead.

Looking around, I saw we'd come out across the yard and into the clump of forest to the back right of the house. We moved away from the shed to get a better look at it.

We circled around, noting it was unremarkable. Basic wood, aged over time. Possibly painted a brown color long ago, which would have made it blend into its surroundings. There was a cluster of tall trees surrounding it on three sides, offering protection from the elements and aid in camouflage. Knowing what it hid inside, I understood the need for secrecy.

"It hadn't felt like we'd walked that far from the house." Pete gestured across the yard.

"No. Let's go back, though, the way we came. I want to go up that staircase we passed and see what part of the house it leads to."

"Do you think the person who killed John and Annie may have gone through the passageway?"

I shrugged. "It's possible."

With that thought in mind, the allure lost some of its appeal. Not enough to scare me off, though.

We circled the shed once more, then headed back inside and secured the door. Pete closed the passageway door behind us as I waited at the bottom of the stairs. Once more, in the dark, we turned on our lights. Soon, after walking a while, we reached the junction and headed up the stairs this time.

We reached the end of the line quickly, and when we pushed against the trapdoor, we found ourselves at the back of a closet. Coming out, I noticed we were in the master bedroom. The room that would have been John and Annie's.

Pete's idea that the killer may have come through the passageway seemed all the more likely.

CHAPTER 13

"Could you imagine if we solved a hundred-year-old murder?" Pete asked, having swallowed a bite of the dinner he'd cooked up.

Surprisingly, it was good.

"Yes, that would be a bonus. But we'd have to forgo any bragging rights, or the new owner may use it against us in court."

Pete smirked. "As soon as I get back to work, I'm going to look into that Costa."

The determined, annoyed look on his face gave me shivers. Not the good kind. But I was grateful to no longer be on his auditor radar.

After dinner, we had coffee in the

sitting room. Pete started a fire in the hearth while I fiddled with my tape recorder. He soon joined me on the couch.

Seeing what I was doing, he looked around. "Are we alone?"

"For now. I am hoping someone will make an appearance so I can ask about the passageway."

We didn't have to wait long. Annie, slow and cautious, crept into the room, seemingly drawn to the fire.

"Hi, Annie." My gentle greeting was for Pete's benefit as well as Annie's. I wasn't sure who was more startled.

Annie's form became more solid as she held her hands toward the flames and acknowledged me with a nod. Casually, I hit the record button on my device. Pete had paled somewhat, and I silently hoped he wouldn't bolt from the room.

"I want to ask you something, Annie. Is that okay?" When she nodded again, I continued. "We found a trapdoor in the back of the cupboard in the kitchen. It led outside to a gardener's shed and also to the bedroom upstairs." I watched her carefully for any signs of emotion. If she showed signs of fear, it may be possible that she recalled her assailant emerging from the closet. But she smiled and appeared thoughtful.

"John told me his dad built this house after he married John's mother. There was a smaller house on the property, nothing more than a shack, really. But he'd come into some money, so he decided to build them a new home. He chose to make it so grand in the hopes of having a large family and even servants one day. Unfortunately, he wound up spending so much on the house that there was no money left at the end."

"It's a lovely home." I knew he'd passed away before his dreams could be realized.

Annie smiled, her memories taking hold. "John's mother loved to work in the garden. That's why the passage leads to the garden shed. In the winter months, if she wanted to go out there, she wouldn't have to trudge through the snow."

"That's nice."

Annie winked at me. "At least, that's what John told me. After talking with John's sisters, I heard the truth of the matter."

"Oh, really?" Now she had me intrigued.

"Apparently, John's dad used to sneak out for a nip in the shed. He'd use the passage in the winter months when John's mom was sitting by a warm fire, not plodding around in a garden shed in the cold." She laughed lightly. "But if that's what John wanted to believe, I saw no harm in letting him."

I had a feeling the 'nip' was whiskey or some other alcoholic drink.

When I laughed along with Annie, Pete stared at me. "What's she saying?"

"Shhh," I said to Pete. "Go on, Annie."

"It helped that the passage also went up to the master bedroom, so if John's dad was late getting to bed, he could sneak in, his wife none the wiser." She looked sad for a moment. "I wish I'd known them. They were both gone before John and I met."

"Such a shame."

"I love gardening, just like John's mother," she told me. "But John didn't keep any spirits out in the shed, so he had no need to be using the passage to go out there in the winter months. Although, on occasion, sometimes, after he and Will returned from the war, they'd both go out there to talk." She swept her gaze around the room as though about to reveal something secretive.

"All that talk about guns, and death, dying…. I didn't like it. It frightened me. I think it frightened them as well, but they seemed obsessed with discussing it. Like it was a part of them. I know my John had terrible nightmares. I even had to shake him sometimes to wake him from them. He'd cry out and thrash about. On a few occasions, he even woke Will, who had to come running from his room and help me with—"

"Who are you talking to?" I heard John interrupt as he glided into the room. He stopped advancing when he saw me and Pete. "Oh, I should have known. The busybodies." He resumed gliding over until he was beside Annie. He took her hands in his. Annie beamed up at him.

"My love," she said.

"Dearest," he replied, leaning to kiss her on the cheek.

"Hi, John. It's nice to see you again." John dropped Annie's hands and eyed me critically.

Pete rose to his feet, his gaze aimed at the hearth as was mine. "Oh great. Look, man to man, John, that possession thing—not cool."

John looked at me. "What is he talking about?"

"You know, darling," Annie said, saving me an explanation. "When we first saw each other again. It was so wonderful.

We were so excited, we flew right into their bodies." Annie looked at me and then Pete. Pete was looking everywhere now and held up his hands like it would prevent a repeat possession.

"We are dreadfully sorry about that," Annie said.

John cleared his throat. "Oh, yes. Dreadfully sorry."

"We got carried away, having not laid eyes on each other in so long," Annie explained.

"They're apologizing," I said to Pete. "It's okay," I assured them.

"No, it's not," Pete argued.

"Why don't you wait for me in the kitchen?" I suggested to Pete. He scampered out of the room before the words finished leaving my mouth.

"What a strange man," Annie observed.

"Never mind him, my love," John said, taking Annie's hands again. "I heard you talking about being frightened."

"Oh," Annie appeared flustered at having been caught sharing something personal about him.

"Annie was just mentioning that you and Will were in the war together. Annie, that must have been lonely for you being here for many years on your own." I said by way of helping her out.

She looked at me gratefully. "Yes. Those were long, frightening years."

"My darling," John said. "I'm so sorry you had to be alone for so long."

She stared up into his eyes. "It's nothing compared to all this time without you. So many years, John. Decades apart. Where were you?"

John was now the one who appeared flustered. "I, I have been searching for Will. I couldn't let his crimes go unpunished."

"You stayed away so long, wrapped up in revenge when we could have been together. We could have moved on." The sorrow in Annie's voice made John appear guilt-ridden.

"I know. I'm sorry. But how can I move on and let Will go unpunished? He killed us. Murdered you in our bed. Then me when I confronted him at the door. I tried to get to you, my love. I tried."

"They found your body at the top of the stairs," I told him gently.

"So close." Annie shook her head sorrowfully.

John turned and stared at the flames. "I remember falling over, succumbing to my wound. Then suddenly, I felt so light, my pain and exhaustion, gone."

"Why did you not come to me?" Annie asked.

"I... I saw you from the doorway. I could not bear to venture further into the room. So much blood. Everywhere. I knew you were gone. Then, I heard the front door slam. Will was getting away. I went after him, but I could not get out the door for some reason. Then I remembered the passageway. Through there, I was able to get outside and go after Will. And I found him. Fallen over at the creek. The knife he used to slay us both was buried in his belly. A fitting end! Though his body lay upon the ground, I saw him lingering nearby. I could see through him, and I knew he was gone, like me. So once more, I chased him. But again, he escaped me. And then I was lost. Searching in the woods for him for so long. I tried to find the gardener's shed, but I could not. The fog, it was so thick, just like in the war. I tried to get back to you, Annie. Yet every time I thought I had found my way home, I was pushed back. Into the woods and the fog."

Annie brushed away ghostly tears and reached for John's hands. "My love, we're together now. The fog has lifted, and you have found me. Please, put away your thoughts of vengeance. Let us move on to the afterlife together."

John looked deeply into Annie's eyes, then disappeared.

"No!" Annie cried, then she, too, disappeared.

"Great." Disappointed, I sat down on the couch and hit the off button on my recorder. Pete peeked around the corner as I rewound the tape.

"All clear?" he asked.

"Yeah, they're gone."

He came over to sit beside me. "How'd it go?"

I sighed. "John is still set on revenge against Will. He refuses to move on until he has it out with him. Annie is devastated."

"Oh no, that sounds terrible."

"It's okay." I smiled.

"It is?"

"Yes. I know what happened. I know who the killer is."

Now, I just had to get Will, John, and Annie into the same place so I could explain everything and cross them over.

Easier said than done.

CHAPTER 14

Everything was set to go. It'd taken a lot of preparation and, of course, persuasion not only with Pete but with Annie as well—my co-conspirators.

Now, three days after our conversation in the sitting room, everything was ready.

"Of course, it has to be at midnight," Pete complained, rubbing his hands together and then running them up and down his thighs to warm them. The biting chill of the night air didn't help his mood any. He'd been quite vocal as we'd dragged out my equipment and put everything into place. I'd been too nervous to feel the cold.

"Stop complaining. If all goes well,

we'll have accomplished what we set out to do. Then we can spend a couple days enjoying the festival in town." It was Friday night. Halloween was in two days. Plus, aiding in tonight's endeavor was the first night of the full moon cycle. A powerful time of year.

Pete and I had decided, after I told him my plan, that we would stick around until Costa took possession of the house. If everything went the way I hoped it would, the ghosts would be crossed over, and I hadn't felt comfortable leaving Janet to explain things alone to the new owner. Pete had assured both Janet and I during our meeting in town that Costa would have a hard time getting any judge to allow a lawsuit based on a lack of ghosts. After combing through Janet's paperwork of the conditions of the sale, there hadn't been any exact mention of ghosts. The only sticking point Pete could find was the phrase *property must be found in the same condition at the date of possession as upon purchase, with contents and 'particulars discussed and agreed upon' intact.* Which he assured us could mean any number of things, not necessarily ghosts.

Janet hadn't seemed well, barely picking at her food at Jimmy's diner. I'd been concerned that her decision to have me cross over the ghosts despite Costa's insistence they remain was wearing on her. She'd been surprised to hear about a secret passageway in her house she'd never known existed. She had promised to stop by sometime later with Lara to investigate it, but we hadn't heard from her, which led to my fear that she really was feeling unwell. When her friend Lara arrived near the end of our discussion, I was relieved we wouldn't be leaving Janet on her own.

Afterward, Pete and I had scoured the area until we found a glass lemonade pitcher that looked almost identical to the one which had broken, just in case Costa added that to his list of things missing in the house.

All my equipment ready, I went into the garden shed and peered down the dark staircase into the passageway.

"Is she here yet?" Pete asked, coming up behind me.

"Not yet. I hope she comes soon, though. Otherwise, this won't work."

Pete looked at his watch. "It's eleven-thirty. Did you tell her what time?"

"It doesn't really work that way. Time doesn't register the same as it does for the dead as it does for the living. I have to give her sight references, like 'after dark.'"

"So how do you know she'll even show up?"

"If she's not here soon, I'll head back into the house this way and see if I can find her."

I'd got the idea to use the passageway from what John had told me. As a ghost, he'd not been able to exit through the front door of the house, but he had been able to use the passage to get outside. If he could do it, I was sure Annie could too. Convincing her had not been easy. Listening to my plan, she'd agreed it may work, but she would be a wary participant.

"Phoebe?" I heard my name whispered from the dark depths of the passageway.

"Annie, I'm here. Just follow my voice."

Since she and John appeared in tune to each other now, I was hoping he would soon follow. And being outside, on neutral ground, may encourage Will to come also.

Pete left the shed, and I followed with Annie. Her reaction to being outside for the first time in over a hundred years was animated. We remained silent, not wanting to rush her. We'd fastened a few overhead lights to tree limbs so the area was still well-lit. Annie's gaze traveled over the land and forest and back to the shed.

"So many memories." Her tone was nostalgic.

If all went well, I hoped she would soon find peace after so many years of loneliness.

After a few minutes, I asked, "Annie, did you get a chance to talk to Will about what we discussed?"

She nodded once, seeming hesitant to speak again.

"Has he agreed to join us?"

"I have," came a deep voice from behind me that wasn't Pete's.

I jumped and turned in that direction.

"Whatsa matter?" Pete hissed, staring all around. "Is there another one?"

"Hi, Will," I greeted, answering Pete's question as well.

Will ignored me and glided over to Annie. He smiled at her obvious pleasure at being outside.

"All the fun times we had out here," she said to Will.

"I remember," he agreed, his tone wistful.

I hated to break up their reminiscing, but time was of the essence. "Will, we know what happened. You need to stop taking responsibility, or John will never come to terms with it."

Will's struggle was visible on his face.

One of the two cameras I had outside on tripods fell over, causing us all to jump.

"What the devil is going on here?" John surged toward Annie, making Will move away.

"Thanks for joining us, John." I kept my voice calm amidst the sudden tension in the air. Catching sight of Will, I held his gaze, silently pleading with him to remain. He looked at Annie, then back at me, and gave a nod.

"What's happening," Pete asked.

"Stand back and wish me luck. They're all here." I waited while he moved closer to the line of trees.

"Why will none of you answer me?" John demanded.

"Darling." Annie reached for John's hands, which he reluctantly allowed her to take. His gaze, however, was darting everywhere.

"We call it an intervention in this time," I said to John.

"Well, I call it someone who doesn't know when to mind their own business," he snapped.

"Please, don't be rude to Phoebe, John. She's here to help us."

"We've found our way back to each other, my love. We don't need any help."

I saw her grip on his hands tighten. "But we do."

He yanked his hands free and flashed an angry glare at Will. "Begone, murdering coward! False friend." As he made a move in Will's direction, Annie darted in front of him.

"No, he is not false. He is a friend of the truest sort," Annie insisted.

I maneuvered to see John's expression,

and as expected, it was of disbelief.

"How, Annie? How can you say that when he murdered you, then turned his weapon upon me? If he hadn't fled and fallen on the knife in his haste, he would have got away. Don't you see? He must pay for his crimes. If not in life, then in death."

Annie shook her head. "No, John. It is you who does not see."

John looked back at Annie, but she turned an imploring gaze on me. "I cannot tell him."

Hesitantly, I moved closer to the pair. "John, what Annie is trying to say is that Will did not kill her. You did."

CHAPTER 15

Furious, John flew up before me, making me cringe from the mask of anger he wore.

"How dare you," he snarled in my face.

I stood my ground. "You were asleep. Having a nightmare about the war. Annie said you had them a lot. You'd yell and thrash about, even waking up Will sometimes, who had to rush to help Annie. But that particular night, there was a terrible storm. Thunder and lightning, rain pelting the house. A catalyst for someone suffering from post-traumatic stress disorder."

"What?" John stared at me scornfully, not allowing my words to penetrate him.

"It's what you would call shellshock in your time. It's a real thing. And people experiencing it can commit unimaginable acts when caught up in an episode."

He shook his head in denial. "Yes, I had nightmares from the war, but none that would make me kill my own wife," he insisted. "This is all a lie Will cooked up to fool you."

"No, John, my darling, it's true."

John turned and went back to Annie, joining their hands again. "Lies, Annie. They're filling your head with terrible lies. Trying to turn you against me."

This time it was Annie who yanked her hands free of his grip. "I remember, John! After talking with Phoebe about the dreams, I remember that night. The thunder waking me up, seeing you standing in the doorway, a flash of lightning illuminating the knife in your hand, you coming toward me, not knowing who I was." A faraway gaze in her eyes, she trembled visibly.

"No," John insisted. "I remember waking to your screams. I was in the parlor, asleep before the fire. I rushed to the stairs, and at the front door, I saw Will, bloody and holding a knife. I charged at him, and he turned the weapon on me."

Will glided forward. "It is true. You did see me standing at the door. I had run across the field, hearing Annie's screams even through the storm. Inside, I heard you yelling in the parlor. I found you there, covered in blood, holding the knife. You were still in the throes of a terrible nightmare, and I feared you had finally done the unthinkable. You came at me, believing I was the enemy. We struggled, covering me in the blood as well. I got the knife from you. I ran for the front door, fearing it was too late for Annie—there was so much blood. I meant to throw the knife outside, where it could do no more harm, and then to check on her, but as I opened the door, you saw me there. Finally awakened, you came forward, startling me, screaming that I'd killed Annie. When I turned, you ran right into the knife. I did not know if you would survive, but if you did, I knew it would destroy you to learn what you had done. I ran, but I fell. The next thing I knew, I was standing at the creek, and then I saw you. At first, I rejoiced, thinking you were all right, but as you came closer, I saw right through you. I looked down at my own hands and saw through them as well. And then, at the creek, I saw my body fallen. And I knew the knife had killed us all. God forgive me, but I ran away, unable to face you. I failed you, my friend, in your greatest time of need."

John's hands went to his ears. "I will hear no more of your lies."

"They are not lies, John," Annie insisted.

"He's telling the truth," I said.

"Look me in the face," Will said. "And know what I say is true."

John lowered his hands and looked

at him. "Then why, why say that you are guilty?"

Will held his gaze. "Am I not? Guilty of being too late, guilty of not saving you both, guilty of killing you, John?"

"That was an accident," I reminded him.

"All the same, I am guilty. In my failure, I could at least give you peace. Free you from facing the demons of what you had done. It was not your fault," Will insisted.

"Nor was it yours," Annie assured Will gently.

"No. I cannot believe what you say is true," John said. "The alternative is too horrible to imagine."

Annie glided over so that she was beside Will. "I know the truth of the matter now, John. It was shocking for me as well, but I know you did not mean to do it."

"No," John continued in his denial, gaze fixated on the pair.

"I forgive you, John," Annie told him,

her tone loving and sad. "But know this, I am ready to move on into the afterlife. If you cannot accept what is true, you will not move on. Do you not want to be together for eternity, my love?"

As if on cue, a brilliant white light appeared, encircling Annie and Will. Appearing fearful, John moved back.

"I cannot…." John's declaration was filled with despair.

"As hard as it is to face it, you must," I added my voice to reason. Time was running out.

Tears ran down Annie's face.

"John," I said, desperate for him not to be left behind, "please, accept the truth." It surprised me when I felt someone take my hand, and I noticed Pete beside me.

John locked eyes with Will. "Swear an oath. Tell me what you have revealed is true."

Will, never breaking eye contact, nodded once. "I swear it. You know I am ever your brother and dearest friend. You saved my life once in the war. Do you remember?"

A trace of a smile curled the corners of John's lips. "Yes, I remember it well."

"And after the war, when I had no one, you brought me with you. Gave me a home, made me part of your family."

"Yes."

"I would never harm you or Annie." Will's admission was barely a whisper. He reached out his hand to John. Then Annie reached out as well.

There was a collective sigh when John finally took both their hands and stepped into the light. The trio shared a fond gaze with each other, finally knowing and accepting the truth of their demise. Then they turned their gazes upon Pete and me.

"Thank you, Phoebe," Annie said. The men each gave a gracious nod acknowledging me.

And then they were gone.

My long sigh caused Pete to squeeze

my hand again. "Did it work?" he asked out of the corner of his mouth.

I nodded and, over the lump in my throat, said, "They're gone."

He pulled me into his arms and kissed the top of my head. "Oh, thank God. Can we go inside now? I'm freezing."

I smiled, fully back in the land of the living. "Yes." We pulled apart, and I rubbed my hands together.

Later, after we packed up the equipment and brought it inside, we went into the sitting room, and Pete made a fire before sitting down on the sofa. Standing before the warm flames, I couldn't help but think about John and Will in here all those years ago. I lit three candles on the mantle, whispering, 'Godspeed,' relieved things had at last worked out for the long-dead residents.

"It's ready." Pete put the tape recorder on the table and waited until I sat down with him.

His face was animated as we listened. It was faint, but the recorder had picked up most of tonight's conversation.

"It'll be great if we got some good video from this as well." My newest camera was state of the art, and if it picked up images of the ghosts and especially the beam of heavenly light, it could make my career. Thankfully, that camera hadn't been the one knocked to the ground.

When the tape was finished, I rewound it and set the recorder aside. "I'm so happy things worked out. It was really tense there at the end, you know?" I'd told Pete about the white light, and he'd been properly amazed.

"I'm so tired all of a sudden. I guess now that it's over and...." I stopped talking and stared at Pete, whose gaze was all over the place. "Hey, are you okay?"

He didn't look at me. "Sure, yeah, whatever, I'm fine."

"Are you... crying?"

CHAPTER 16

We slept in late on Saturday, and since the weather was fine, we strolled to Jimmy's and had pancakes and coffee. Near the end of brunch, I saw Lara come in and pick up an order to go at the counter.

"Hi, Lara," I called from our table, hoping for a chance to speak to her before she rushed off.

Seeing me, she smiled and came over. "Hi, Phoebe, Pete." She seemed distracted and fidgeted with the paper bag in her hands.

"How's Janet doing?"

"Oh, that's why I'm here." She lifted the bag up. "Her favorite, blueberry turnovers. I'm hoping I can coax her to eat. I did manage to get some of my chicken soup into her for dinner last night."

Her smile was strained, and I could see the worry on her face.

"Have you called the doctor?" Pete asked.

Lara chuckled. "Not yet. She would not appreciate all that fuss. But between us, if she isn't better by dinnertime tonight, I'm taking her to the hospital."

"The hospital. Do you think it's serious?" I asked.

"At our age, you never know. I do think a night spent with IV fluids may force some sense into her, though. Whenever I comment about her pale complexion or lack of energy, she waves me off.

"She'll be so disappointed to miss the festival," I said.

Lara nodded in agreement. "Every year we go together. This'll be the first time we miss it."

"You're welcome to hang around with us," Pete said.

She smiled at his offer. "Thanks, but I don't want to leave Janet alone. How's things at the house." I saw her look over at Grace, who was covertly wiping down tables around ours.

"All wrapped up. Could you pass that information along to Janet? We thought we'd hang around, though, catch the festival, and be here when the new owner takes possession."

Lara nodded conspiratorially, and I figured Janet had filled her in on Costa's insistence the house be haunted when she turned over the keys.

"She'll appreciate the backup, dear," Lara assured me.

"Between us," I kept my voice low so Grace wouldn't overhear, "I believe something else may still be lurking around there that wants nothing to do with our help."

Lara's face brightened somewhat. "Oh! Well, that just may solve the problem, then."

"Please tell Janet we're thinking of her," Pete said.

"Yes, and if you need anything at all, she has my cell number, and of course, you can call the house as well," I said.

"Thank you. I'll keep that in mind. Goodbye, and enjoy the festival." Lara gave us both a tight smile and headed off.

Grace rushed over to top up our coffees. "I hear Janet's feeling poorly. I hope she'll be all right," she said, looking at me pointedly for information.

"We hope so, too," was all I said. I picked up my coffee, and she wandered off.

Pete had grabbed a paper from the stand on the way in, and now he perused the contents.

"There's a lot going on today. Throughout the park, they'll have a bunch of Halloween-themed activities like a giant hay maze, and there'll be a pumpkin carving and decoration station, or you can stuff a straw person for your stoop. They'll have craft tables set up for the kiddos too. Also, some stores will be putting out tables selling baked goods, crafted items like knitted hats and gloves and scarves, and of course, candy apples. Looks like there will even be a hotdog vendor set up. Oh, and a band too."

"Wow, they're really going all out."

We exchanged a glance and whispered, "Small towns."

"When's everything starting?"

Pete stared at the paper again. "Today, it begins at noon and goes till nine PM. Tomorrow, Halloween, it runs from eleven till three. I'm guessing so everyone can get ready for the trick-or-treaters."

"Do you want to wander through the park today and go again tomorrow?" I was worried he might be anxious to get back home. I knew I was asking a lot of him to stick around and make sure everything went okay with Costa.

He appeared surprised by my question. "Yes. I want to soak it all in. I love this town spirit, getting together to celebrate a holiday. I'd love to see how they do up Christmas here."

"Really?"

"Yeah. You know, I grew up in a large city. My parents and younger brother. We lived in a two-floor condo."

"Sounds nice."

He chuckled. "It was awful. I barely had a handful of friends. My parents and brother were the same. Everyone kept to themselves. There was no sense of community. Not like here." His tone was wistful.

"It was the same with me. But I was an only child living with my parents in an apartment not much bigger than the one I'm in now. The city's not so bad, in a way. Everything's close by, within walking distance, or a short drive. And you'd be amazed how many haunted buildings there are."

He smirked. "I can only imagine."

"But you're right. It always felt like things were rushing by when I was growing up. People were always busy. There was always school and activities. It's all a blur. I don't remember us going on picnics or strolling through a park. We went to the seaside a couple of times, and that was great, but it was for vacations, which were few and far between."

"Yeah, I remember my dad working all the time. My mom had many *social obligations,* so we got left with a nanny a lot."

"A nanny would have been nice company. My mom worked part-time when I was too little to be left alone. She and my dad would swap off duties when he got in from work. I barely saw them together. And then when I was nine, she took a full-time job, and I remember being told to not answer the door for anyone." I didn't tell him how

I'd been afraid back then.

I'd told my parents about talking to ghosts in the building up until the time I figured out it wasn't a normal thing. I'd overheard them complain, when they passed each other like ships in the night, about the possibility of having to pay for a shrink on top of everything else, so I stopped talking about it. There'd been an array of ghosts in our building. Most of them ignored me or didn't hang out much. But there'd been a particular ghost who'd enjoyed scaring me. And after talking to an old woman in the building who'd been kind to me and knew a thing or two about the afterlife, she'd told me about crossing ghosts over to the other side. It'd become an obsession with me, and I remember making it my mission to cross that mean ghost over. In the end, I'd been successful, and what had ensued was an obsession to cross over as many ghosts as I could.

Now finished with our coffees, Pete

gestured to Grace, who came by with the check. "I'll get it," he insisted and left a generous tip on the table as well.

We pulled on our coats and headed out, the park a short walk away. As we got close, I heard voices and music and the laughter of children. The park appeared to sit smack-dab in the middle of town. Already, things were in full swing.

We strolled the grounds, hand in hand, soaking in the atmosphere. Pete stopped at the pumpkin station, where you could opt to traditionally carve a face or design. Or, set at the other end of the table was an array of natural items you could use to decorate one. There was a special paste to use as 'glue' for attaching the items, which, according to the sign, was safe for animals to consume. Several kinds of nuts, pinecones, seeds, and plants were available to choose from. A little girl was using strands of dried grass and straw as hair, set around a decorative face she'd created.

"What a great idea," Pete said. "Then you can toss it in the forest or your yard for wild animals to enjoy after Halloween." The little girl smiled up at him, and he gave her a wink.

"Yes, it is." Seeing the excitement on his face, I asked if he'd like to make one up.

"Maybe on the way out. Still, lots to see and do."

Throughout the next hour, Pete displayed a childlike excitement I found myself getting caught up in. Seeing him this way, relaxed and at peace with the world, was a whole new side to him I never imagined existed.

He caught me staring at him as he munched on a candy apple, half of it stuck to his face and even a piece in his hair. "What? Do I have some on me?"

"No, you're fine. I'm glad you're having a good time. It's nice to see."

He smiled, revealing red teeth. "I am having fun. Are you?" The notion appeared to surprise him.

I nodded. "I am."

"Good. I think it's about time for both of us."

"I've never hung around like this after a job. Although, I've always been on my own."

He put his arm around me, and I tried not to think about the way his hand stuck to my jacket. "I think we've both spent too much time on our own. We should change that."

I stared up into his handsome face, wondering if he was toying with me, but I detected only sincerity. "How?"

He shrugged as though the answer was simple. "We should be together."

"Really?" I was not opposed to the idea. I liked his company, which surprised me. And over the past few days, I'd grown accustomed to his presence. "I'd like that."

"It's settled then. When we get back home, let's date."

"Sounds like a plan."

Chapter 17

Monday morning had arrived, and Costa was due to pull into the driveway at any moment. Janet's realtor had come by earlier and handed us some paperwork when Janet failed to turn up. He'd apologize about not sticking around, explaining that his wife was under the weather and he was tasked with handling their two toddlers. I'd told him we understood and would call if there were any questions or problems.

"What do you think is taking her so long?" I paced while Pete sat at the kitchen table, watching me.

"I'm sure Lara would have called if there was a problem. She was feeling better yesterday, right?"

"Yes." I'd talked with Janet on the phone. She'd assured me she was on the mend and would be out of bed soon. When I'd filled her in on the details of crossing over the ghostly trio, she'd been so relieved. Since she was on bed rest, she asked if Pete and I could pack up some clothing and a few items she'd not gotten to yet. Lara had swung by to pick everything up, and Pete went with her to Janet's storage unit and unloaded it all. There hadn't been much there, he'd relayed to me upon his return, considering she planned to move into the retirement home in town soon. Lara had hinted she had been thinking of doing the same since she was finding it hard to keep her house going on her own.

When Costa pulled up with his realtor, Pete and I were ready to meet them. Janet's realtor had told us he'd explained the circumstances of his absence to Costa's realtor, so we didn't have that worry.

"Where is she?" Costa asked as he came through the door.

I assumed he meant Janet. "She's not here."

"She's been sick," Pete informed him, his look daring Costa to start any trouble.

"We have the keys and the paperwork to hand over," I said. "Everything is in order."

Costa stared around the house. "I'll be the judge of that." He looked at the front door they'd come through, which he'd deliberately left ajar. When it failed to slam shut, he finally closed it. He narrowed his gaze and headed to the staircase. Moving systematically through the second floor, he went up into the attic next. Pete, his realtor, and me followed along.

In the middle of the attic floor, he stretched his hands wide and turned in a slow circle. "Nothing," he snapped. "There's nothing." He turned his frowning face on me. "Where are my ghosts?"

When Pete looked about ready to tell him off, I said, "I assure you, there is still something unnatural in this house." I didn't like the way he looked at Pete. "On Halloween night, things were flying off shelves all over the place." It was the truth.

His poor realtor stood there staring between us, no doubt thinking we were nuts.

"Phoebe?" Janet's voice called out behind me. I turned around, worried she was about to walk in on a fight.

After a moment, all I managed to say was, "Um."

"Um?" Costa snarled. "That's all you have to say for yourself? I'm calling my lawyer." He stormed off toward the stairs, his realtor trailing him.

My gaze remained glued to Janet until I felt Pete come up beside me.

"Hey, don't worry about him, okay? I'm not going to let him do anything to hurt you or Janet."

My cell phone rang suddenly, and I answered it. "Hello?"

"Phoebe? It's Lara. I'm at home and… Janet…" She said between sobs.

"She's gone," I said.

"Yes. Just now. I'm sorry I meant to call earlier, but I knew she was fading, and I called the ambulance. They didn't make it in time."

"It's okay, she's okay," I said.

"She's okay? She'd dead," Lara said.

"No, no, I mean she's here. She's with me in the attic," I explained.

The line was silent for so long that I thought she'd hung up. Then, "She's in the attic. Oh, no. She's stuck there? In the house?"

"Tell her I'll move on soon," Janet said to me with a wink.

I nodded. "She'll be fine. I'll see to it." I listened to Janet's words, then continued to Lara, "She wants to say thank you for all you've done for her and for being her friend."

Lara sobbed into the phone. "Tell her I love her."

"I will," I promised and heard the line click.

Pete stared at me strangely.

"Janet's gone, but she's okay," I told him gently, worried he'd cry again.

He swallowed hard. "She's here now?"

I nodded.

"I'm sorry," I said to Janet.

She shrugged. A black blur suddenly flew across the room and dove into her arms. It was a huge black cat. Janet's face lit up, and she cuddled him and kissed him.

At last, the sinister, elusive presence explained, and I couldn't help but laugh.

"What?" Pete said, his gaze darting everywhere.

"It's a cat, Janet's cat," I explained.

Pete looked confused for a second, then he laughed as well. "That explains things flying off shelves."

"I had a feeling Cinders was here," Janet said. "It's why I came back. Well, for him, and to deal with Mr. Costa. I couldn't leave you holding the bag, Phoebe. Not after you crossed over those poor ghosts."

"Oh, well, thanks. I appreciate that."

"What?" Pete said out of the corner of his mouth. "What's she saying?"

I smiled at Janet conspiratorially and said to him, "She wants to have a little fun with Costa before she goes."

Pete smiled too. "Well, let's not keep him waiting then."

Together, we left the attic.

~*~

One Year Later...

"Ready?" Everything was packed into the car, but I still sat waiting.

Pete came out of the house and down the front porch, a leather case in one hand, a backpack hanging off his shoulder, and a coffee in his hand. He jumped into the passenger side of my jeep and said, "Let's go."

It wasn't like we were going far. Just the other side of town where apparently, a pair of nasty poltergeists were causing trouble in one of the old homes. This town was full of them. Ever since we'd moved here — into Lara's old farmhouse when she put it up for sale — it'd been non-stop job after job.

"Sheesh, you'd think they'd take a break on weekends," Pete said.

He could act all put out as much as he wanted, but I knew he loved coming along with me to these haunts. I didn't want to hurt his feelings by telling him he was welcome to stay home.

"Do you plan on working while we're there?" I asked as he tucked his bags into the back seat.

He shrugged. "May as well be useful. After the equipment's set up, there's not much for me to do."

"Well, I appreciate your help." Sometimes I thought he might be afraid to be alone in the big old house we owned together. It'd taken some getting used to after we'd lived together in my tiny apartment for six months. He'd moved in three months after we'd got home from our first job here. We'd married the weekend before that and spent our honeymoon at the haunted B&B that Costa owned for old-time's sake.

Costa actually turned out to be a pretty decent guy. Especially after we'd revealed the hidden passageway to him. And once he'd been scared silly by Janet and Cinders before I discreetly crossed them over.

We really hadn't needed to worry about a lack of ghosts in the house. Once Annie, John, and Will were gone, a bevy of strange things — according to Costa's weekly article in the Emerald Times — made sure his business had a steady stream of guests. I guess the original trio of ghosts leaving cleared the way for others to arrive. I'd even had to head down there many a night to help out when certain spirits became too noisy or terrifying for the guests.

Pete and I made a good team. In business as well as personally.

It was a strange, exciting life we led. But we were happy.

And I wouldn't change any of it.

Julie is a long-time resident of Hamilton, Ontario, where she lives with her husband of 25 years. She has two grown sons who recently left the nest. Working in a library for several years inspired her to pursue her long-time love of writing.

Please check out her website http://www.julieparker.net